I wasn't happy when I realized I needed to visit the washhouse before sleep would return. I told my bladder to stop hurting, but it didn't. I sighed mightily, threw my sleeping bag aside and slid over the edge of the bed. My feet touched the floor at the same time something (not me) scraped in the dark.

A quick intake of breath followed the noise, then a rush of movement and the creak of a bunk. Someone had bumped into something on the floor—a suitcase, a book—someone moved quietly, too quietly, someone trying to get back to bed before I saw her.

"Who's there?" I whispered.

No one answered.

I listened for more noise, for some natural activity from someone awake like I was. I'd heard lots of girls move around a cabin in the night, and none of them had been as sneaky as this.

I realized that I was listening so hard that I had my eyes squeezed shut. I opened them cautiously and looked around. The interior of the cabin was deep in shadows.

The East Edge Mysteries
- The Secret of the Burning House
- Discovery at Denny's Deli
- Mystery at Harmony Hill

MYSTERY AT
HARMONY HILL

GAYLE ROPER

Chariot Books™
David C. Cook Publishing Co.

Published by Chariot Books™,
an imprint of Chariot Family Publishing
Cook Communications Ministries, Elgin, Illinois 60120
Cook Communications Ministries, Paris, Ontario
Kingsway Communications, Eastbourne, England

MYSTERY AT HARMONY HILL
© 1993 by Gayle G. Roper

Cover illustration by Cindy Webber
Cover design by Helen Lannis
First printing, 1993
Printed in the United States of America
97 96 95 94   5 4 3 2

Library of Congress Cataloging-in-Publication Data
Roper, Gayle G.
Mystery at Harmony Hill/by Gayle Roper.
   p. cm. — (East Edge mysteries : 3.)
Summary: Twelve-year-old Shannon's belief in God's love helps her
when she has to share a cabin at Camp Harmony Hill with several
unfriendly girls and when things begin disappearing from the cabin.
ISBN 1-55513-701-6
[1. Church camps—Fiction. 2. Camps—Fiction. 3. Behavior—
Fiction. 4. Christian life—Fiction. 5. Mystery and detective
stories.]   I. Title.   II. Series: Roper, Gayle G.   East Edge
mystery: 3.
PZ7.R6788My   1993
[Fic]—dc20   92-27105
                                       CIP
                                       AC

I rushed up the steps to Main House. I was so glad to be at Camp Harmony Hill at last that I could hardly stand it.

"Shannon Symmonds," I told the registrar. At least I assumed she was the registrar. She was sitting in the right chair in the right room. She was just a different person than I'd expected to see. "Where's Miss Naomi?"

The woman smiled. "She got married and moved away. I'm Miss Julie, the new registrar."

I nodded. "I thought so. You're in the right place."

Miss Julie gave me a strange look.

"The registrar always sits at this desk on this chair in this room," I explained. "And Miss Dottie always sits at that desk on that chair"—I pointed across the room—"to collect the money we deposit in the camp bank. And she always writes everything on those little 3" x 5" cards."

One of the things that made coming back to Harmony Hill every summer feel like coming home was that nothing ever seemed to change, even when it changed. Like Miss Julie being registrar. Wrong person, right place, so it felt like nothing was different even when it was.

I looked around Main House. Same white walls. Same dark green floors and window frames. Same plants growing on the window sills. Even the same magazines by the chair where visitors sat. 1985 editions, all of them. It was sort of interesting to look at them and see what people had been doing and looking like when I was just a tiny kid.

"What did you say your name was?" Miss Julie asked, still looking up at me with that funny expression.

"Shannon Symmonds," I said. "I was supposed to come for two weeks, but I got sick at the last minute and had to cancel out for last week. But I'm well now."

I straightened to my five feet, eight inches to show her how fit I was. The truth was that I'd been feeling good since Monday, but Mom made me stay home all week just to be certain. I know she's like that because she loves me, but somehow I've got to break her of this overprotection. After all, I'm eleven, going on twelve in January.

"We wouldn't want you to get sick at camp now, would we?" she'd kept saying.

And I'd kept saying, "Why not? I can throw up anywhere, and Harmony Hill would be a more fun place to throw up than home."

"Even in the middle of the night?" Mom had said. "When you have to walk across that dark field to the washhouse?"

She'd had a point there. Racing to the wash house at night wasn't fun even when you were well.

I stood patiently in front of the new registrar waiting for my cabin assignment. All of my crowd from East Edge were staying together. I expected it was too much to hope that the others had saved me a top bunk. Friendship only goes so far, especially when you're sick at home and can't loom over your friends like a vulture—something I do very well since I'm so tall.

Miss Julie's face was buried in her files, and she kept rooting through them as though she'd never seen them before. In the meantime, girls and their parents were lining up behind Mom and me. I frowned slightly, wondering what the holdup was.

"Excuse me a minute," mumbled Miss Julie, and she rushed across the room toward The Main Office.

I looked at Mom. Both of us were frowning now. No one went to The Main Office unless there was a problem.

That was where the director of Harmony Hill, Mrs. Allenwood, sat at her desk. Several times a day she walked around camp, talking with counselors and campers, laughing and being pleasant. But if someone had to go to the office to talk to Mrs. Allenwood, it meant trouble of some kind. That's why everyone said "The Main Office" with capital letters.

Soon Miss Julie and Mrs. Allenwood came out of The Main Office together.

"Hello, Shannon," said Mrs. A. "How nice to see you again."

I smiled. There was something about Mrs. A. that made you feel very warm when she spoke to you. It was as though you were the most important person in the world—unless, of course, you were being disciplined. Then all that energy was still focused on you, but it was ice instead of warmth.

"Are you feeling quite well now?" Mrs. A. asked.

I nodded.

"Well, we need to have a little talk, dear, you and I and your mother."

A funny feeling erupted in my stomach. Something was definitely wrong. I threw a panicky look at Mom.

"What's the problem?" asked Mom, who only came to my chin. She slid her arm around my waist, something she did a lot. It usually made me squirm, but somehow it felt very comforting now. "Is there some confusion about Shannon's registration?"

Mrs. A. smiled and walked across the room, and we followed. I hesitated at the door to The Main Office. I'd never been inside before, and I was half afraid to enter.

"Come on in, Shannon," Mrs. A. said with her warm smile.

I held my breath and prepared to step over the threshold when a very loud voice distracted all three of us—and everyone else in the room.

"That's all you're leaving me?" A girl with long blond hair and long fingernails polished bright red stood by the camp bank table yelling at a woman who had to be her mother. The two looked very much alike because the daughter was trying to look older and the mother was trying to look younger. "I need more money than that!"

"Where are you going to spend it?" her mother asked angrily, waving her hand around the room. "Or are you planning to make me something in the craft shop?"

"I'm only here because I haven't got a choice!" yelled the blond. "The least you can do is leave me some money!"

As I watched with interest, Mrs. Allenwood moved quickly to the bank table and took charge.

"Come on, Nosy." Mom took me by the arm. "The last thing Mrs. Allenwood needs is everyone watching." She dragged me into The Main Office.

"I want to see what happens," I complained. "And by the way, I hope you plan to leave me lots of money."

"I'm sorry," said Mom. "I only have a million on me."

"Cheapskate," I said as Mrs. Allenwood returned.

Mom and I sat facing Mrs. A. with her big metal desk, neat and clear of papers, between us. She laced her fingers together and smiled.

"Mrs. Symmonds, it seems Miss Julie wasn't expecting Shannon today. When you canceled her registration due to her illness last week, Miss Julie thought the cancellation was for the entire two-week period."

"Oh, no," said Mom. "I'm certain I only canceled one week. I knew Shannon would be well soon. She only had a virus."

There was a knock on the door.

"Come in," called Mrs. A.

Miss Julie entered hesitantly, a folder in her hand. She handed it to Mrs. A. and almost raced back to her own desk.

Mrs. A. opened the folder and lifted out a paper. It was my camp registration. From my seat I could read my name on the top line because Mom had written it with a heavy black marker. A little yellow Post-it was attached.

Mrs. A. turned the form with its little note toward Mom and me. The note said, "Canceled due to illness."

My stomach felt worse that it had when I had the virus.

"Does this mean I can't stay?" I asked, trying not to sound too upset.

"Oh, no," said Mrs. A., smiling warmly.

I instantly felt better.

"But," she continued, "I wanted to talk with you because this confusion has created a small difficulty."

My stomach cramped again.

"Redwood Cabin, where your friends are, is full of girls who have been here for a week already, and they're all staying for a second week. I'm sure you understand that we can't move them."

I hate it when people say, "I'm sure you understand." How can you say, "No, I don't understand. I think the situation stinks! Change it!"?

"But what about my bed?" I asked. "The one I was supposed to have had last Saturday?"

"We filled it with a girl who wanted to come at the last minute."

"Well, can't you move her?" I asked. How could I not be in a cabin with Cammi and Dee and Alysha and Bethany?

Mrs. A. leaned over her desk toward me. "I know you must be terribly upset, my dear. I know I would be if I were you. But there's a bunk in Ponderosa Cabin that's yours if you want it."

I looked at Mom. I was so disappointed I could hardly think.

"You're only in your cabin at night," Mom said. "You can hang around with the girls all day."

I shook my head. I couldn't hang around with the girls all day. So many things were scheduled by cabin that it'd only be luck if I was ever at the same place at the same time as the others.

"Shannon," said Mrs. A., "many of our girls come to camp knowing no one. If they can manage it, I'm sure someone of your caliber certainly can."

Uh-oh. Another of those adult phrases: "Someone of your caliber." But the compliment sounded so good, I let her manipulate me. Especially when the only other choice—going home—was worse.

"Ponderosa Cabin will be fine," I said in my best martyr voice. I got slowly to my feet and dragged myself to the door.

I saw Mom and Mrs. A. exchange glances.

Well, I thought, *let them worry about me and wonder how sad and disappointed I am. Because, truth to tell, I AM NOT THRILLED!*

I dragged my suitcase up the steps to Ponderosa, carefully bumping it on every riser. Out of the corner of my eye, I could see Mom wince with every bump, so I bounced the thing harder. The more scratches and marks, the better I would feel.

I should be flying into Redwood, not bumping into Ponderosa, for Pete's sake! It was unfair enough that I had to get sick—and I never get sick. It was beyond unfair that I was now stuck in a cabin with a bunch of people I'd never seen before in my life and had no desire to see.

I pulled the screen door open and walked into my home for the next week. I hated it already.

It looked just like every other cabin at Harmony Hill, with its five bunk beds and one single bed for the counselor lining the walls. The top half of the cabin was screened, with rolled-up canvas awnings on the outside to lower when it rained.

I was secretly delighted to see that a top bunk against the back wall was still vacant, but I kept my woe-is-me face carefully in place as I spread my sleeping bag. I put my Bible, notebook, and flashlight on my pillow and shoved the suitcase under the bed. I was all moved in.

Only then did I turn around to meet my counselor.

"Hi," said a slightly plump redhead.

She wore flowered shorts and a bright pink T-shirt that said "Camp Harmony Hill" across the back. Between her hair and the shirt, she was brilliant enough to be a beacon on a dark, stormy night.

"I'm Dorian." She smiled warmly.

I sighed inside. I had been hoping I'd at least get a counselor I knew from other summers. Then maybe I wouldn't feel quite so lost.

Not that Dorian didn't look nice. Her smile was the warm, toasty kind. She was probably fine. It's just that she was just a stranger, and I wanted someone I knew.

While Mom and I stood with Dorian, the cabin door banged open and in marched the girl with the long blond hair who had been screaming for more money at Main House. She stood in the middle of the room and frowned as she looked around. I'm sure I heard her snort in disgust.

Suddenly I felt very protective toward Ponderosa.

"Hi, I'm Dorian," said Dorian to the new girl. "I'll be your counselor this week, and I'm so glad you're here." She smiled her wonderful smile.

"Well, I'm not!" The girl stared at her mother, who stared right back. I wondered if they often had these contests, and if so, who blinked first most of the time. I was willing to bet that it wasn't the girl.

This time the mother blinked first. She turned to Dorian and smiled sweetly.

"Don't let Tracy distress you," she said warmly. "She'll be fine once she gets settled." She turned back to her daughter, and her smile disappeared and her voice became cold. "We'll see you next Saturday. If you need anything, call Grandma."

With those words, Tracy's mother turned and quickly followed Tracy's father out of the cabin. He had been standing quietly in the doorway, boredom oozing from every pore. They walked across the playing field, past the pool, and into the parking lot without ever looking back. They never even said good-bye.

I glanced at Tracy, who stood like a statue. Her face was white and her eyes were slits of anger and hurt.

Dorian cleared her throat. "Why don't you pick a bunk, Tracy? If there's no sleeping bag on it, it's available."

Tracy looked at Dorian with dislike, then spun around and headed for the nearest bottom bunk—which, thankfully, wasn't below my bed.

Mom put her hand on my arm and gestured with her head toward the door. "Want an ice-cream cone before I leave?"

I nodded. It had become a Harmony Hill ritual to get a huge cone before Mom left, because Saturday afternoon was the one day the camp store didn't limit what we could buy. And the money came out of Mom's pocket, not my allowance.

As I walked Mom to the car, I licked and slurped at my three dips of rocky road while Mom nibbled daintily at a baby-sized scoop of vanilla that was so small it only cost a quarter.

By the time Mom rolled down her car window to kiss me good-bye, I wasn't upset about Redwood anymore. I wouldn't say I was looking forward to a week in Ponderosa with Tracy, but I never have been able to stay angry or upset for very long. A little ice cream, some fresh air, and Mom's obvious worry on my behalf had made me feel much better. I was actually smiling as I walked back to the cabin area.

I went to Redwood to look for my friends. Cammi, Alysha, Bethany, and Dee are members with me of the Kids Care Club. We all go to the same school and the same church, and we work to earn extra money for ourselves and our church by helping people with different small jobs.

I raced up the steps of their cabin and threw the door open. "You can start to enjoy yourselves now," I announced. "I'm here."

Three surprised faces looked at me, and I'd never seen any of them before in my life.

"Hooray," said one of them sarcastically. "I'm so excited."

Heat poured into my face, and I knew I must be scarlet with embarrassment.

"Where are Dee and Alysha and Bethany and Cammi?" I asked.

"I have no idea," said the sarcastic girl. "Fortunately for them."

Lovely girl, I thought. *She must be a wonderful*

cabinmate. We should put her in with Tracy.

"When they get back, tell them Shannon's here, okay?" I said. I didn't wait for an answer.

All the cabins stood in a line at the edge of the large open field, just under a canopy of pine trees. Three tetherball games were set up by the cabins. I walked to the one nearest my cabin and began batting the ball, counting how many swats it took to make it wrap itself around its pole.

The door of Ponderosa slammed. I glanced up and saw a girl almost as tall as I am. She had lots of dark curly hair and dark, dark eyes. She stood on the porch of our cabin and watched me punch the ball.

"Want to play?" I asked.

"Play?" she said. "Aren't we a little old for playing?"

I shrugged. "I don't think so. After all, grown men 'play' baseball and football and basketball and make huge fortunes doing it."

I swung at the ball with all my might and just tipped it as it flew by.

"Here," the girl on the porch said, her voice dripping with disgust. "Let me show you how it's done."

Much to my surprise, she was good, and we

19

had a great time. When we paused between games, I looked at my sore, red fist.

"It hurts," I said, rubbing it.

"Wimp," she said, but in a joking voice.

"I'm Shannon," I said.

"I'm Charlie."

"Is that a nickname for Charlotte?"

She shook her head. "My real name's Charlette. With a 'ch' sound like church."

"I never heard that name before."

"I tell my mom she must have made it up," laughed Charlie.

"Where do you live?" I asked.

She shrugged. "Here and there. How about you?"

"East Edge."

She looked at me sharply, like what I had said was important, but she didn't comment.

"Have you been to Harmony Hill before?" I asked to keep the conversation going.

"Never. And I would have been happy keeping it that way."

That was two for two. Would I meet anyone in Ponderosa who was happy to be here?

"We have to play a tie-breaker," she said. She had won three games so far and so had I.

She socked the ball and it flew through the air, wrapping itself rapidly about the pole. I swiped at it and missed. I raised my hand, knowing I couldn't afford to miss again.

"Shannon! Look! It's Shannon!"

I spun around at the welcome sound of Alysha's voice. The tetherball whipped past me unnoticed as my friends ran up to me, yelling and cheering.

I barely heard Charlie say, "I won."

"So tomorrow is Easter, Monday is Valentine's Day, Tuesday is Thanksgiving, Wednesday is Christmas, Thursday is the Fourth of July, and Friday is Birthday Day." Dorian grinned and looked around Ponderosa.

I found myself grinning back. She was going to be okay as a counselor, I could tell. Anyone who could make the Saturday afternoon get-acquainted meeting exciting had to be good.

Besides that ray of sunshine, Tracy, and Charlie, who had the bunk beneath mine, there were seven other girls in the cabin. Two mousy girls had come together. They spoke so softly I hadn't even been able to hear their names when they introduced themselves. Then there were five girls who had come together all the way from New Jersey. They made me sad because they reminded me that I should be in Redwood with my friends.

Seeing the East Edge girls had been hard. It felt good that they were glad to see me—and they sounded really disappointed that I couldn't be in Redwood with them. "We'll see you around," they said, but we all knew we wouldn't see much of each other.

"We'll give little gifts on Christmas and Birthday Day," Dorian said, her welcome lecture almost finished. "You can make something in the craft shop or buy a candy bar or do whatever you wish. We'll draw names now for both holidays."

I felt excitement bubbling inside. I love Holiday Week because I love celebrations and gifts and special decorations and all that stuff. I'd even brought a huge pad of colored paper, a sketch pad, paste, tape, glitter, felt markers, and scissors with me to make paper chains and collages and Christmas tree ornaments. Of course Harmony Hill provides materials for us, but I always want to make more.

"My budding artist," Mom calls me. I know she's teasing me, but that's exactly what I plan to be someday. When my father left us two years ago, I drew for hours. It was better than crying, and it helped me stay calm. It even helped me pray. I still get a horrible pain in my heart when-ever I think of that time, but I draw my way out.

I pulled Charlie's name for Christmas and Tracy's name for Birthday Day. I thought Charlie would be fine to give to, but I wasn't excited about Tracy. She'd probably stare me down like she did her mother and throw the gift in the trash. With a smile.

"And now I have something else for fun," Dorian said, hopping up from her bed.

Tracy didn't actually make a raspberry sound, but it was close. I felt sorry for the girls whose names she had drawn for Christmas and Birthday Day.

Dorian walked around the cabin and gave us each a piece of paper. I looked at my sheet and found a list for a scavenger hunt:

an oak leaf
moss
a dead branch
a cup of creek water
a footprint
an acorn
golden rod
a skipping stone
two wild berries

a caterpillar
a fern frond
a pinecone
a feather
some mud
a milkweed pod
a red leaf
an insect
briars
a wild strawberry vine
bark from a dead log

"The idea is to find as many of these things as you can in the next thirty minutes," Dorian said. "All the other cabins will be out there looking too. The cabin that finds the most in the least time will get lots of points toward the pizza party Friday night. Only one cabin gets to eat the pizza, and I don't know why Ponderosa can't be the one."

I looked around at my cabinmates while Dorian talked. I didn't share her confidence about that pizza.

Suddenly a whistle sounded outside.

"Ten! Nine! Eight!" yelled Miss Martha, the games director, as she stood on the edge of the field in front of the cabins.

"When she yells GO, girls, you're off!" said Dorian.

I jumped down from my bunk where I'd been lying and started for the door.

"Seven! Six!" yelled Miss Martha.

"I'm not going into any woods," said Tracy flatly. She had been lying on her bunk staring at the ceiling, the picture of boredom. Now she sat up, folded her arms across her chest and looked mutinous. "I hate the outdoors!"

"Five! Four! Three!" yelled Miss Martha.

"Come on, Tracy," said Dorian with a smile. "It'll be great fun."

Tracy looked Dorian in the eye. "Fun? Hah! That's a lie, and you know it."

Dorian blinked in disbelief. So did I. Aside from the fact that I was surprised at Tracy's rudeness (but then again, maybe I wasn't), I really did think the hunt would be fun.

"Anyone who wants to play a stupid game like this is sick!" Tracy's eyes glittered with anger.

"Two! One! GO!" yelled Miss Martha.

Cabins doors slammed and footsteps sounded as girls rushed to find the items on their lists. But our group stood frozen in the middle of Ponderosa, staring at Tracy.

"What's an oak leaf look like?" yelled a girl as she ran by our cabin.

"Who knows?" answered one of her teammates. "We'll just get lots of different kinds, and one's bound to be right."

Their chatter broke the tension for me.

"At least I know what an oak leaf looks like," I said. I clapped my hands like a coach giving a pep talk. "Come on! If Tracy doesn't want to go, we'll have to do it without her."

"Shouldn't be too hard," muttered Charlie under her breath.

I had to fight the giggles.

We all made a break for the door and thundered down the steps and into the woods behind our cabin. Almost immediately one of the mousy girls held up a pinecone, grinning triumphantly.

"Wait a minute!" I yelled. "I'll be right back!"

I raced back to Ponderosa and grabbed the wastebasket.

"We need this to keep our stuff in," I explained to Dorian as I dumped a bunch of dirty tissues on the floor.

She was sitting on her bed staring at Tracy who lay on hers, face to the wall. Dorian's lovely smile was gone, and she nodded absently in my direction.

Poor Dorian! How in the world would she ever manage Tracy?

I dashed back to my team with the basket in hand. The finder of the pinecone, whose name turned out to be Cissy, also had an acorn, and she placed both her contributions carefully in the basket.

"If there's an acorn, there has to be an oak leaf," I said. Once again Cissy came through, waving the lobed leaf proudly.

"I've got a dead branch," said Charlie, holding up a huge limb.

"I don't think it has to be that big," I said.

She shrugged. "Can it be this big?"

"I guess."

"Then we have a dead branch." Charlie dragged it behind her as we followed the path deeper into the woods.

"There's the creek," said Cissy. "What shall we put the water in?"

"How about our wastebasket?" suggested her timid friend, Leigh.

The two of them grabbed the basket from me and raced down a slight incline to the creek. They dumped our already found treasures out and scooped up some water.

"What do we do tomorrow to make it Easter?" Charlie asked. She was standing beside me with her eyes on Cissy and Leigh, but there was an urgent quality to her question. "Does the Easter bunny come? We're not supposed to have fancy dresses or anything, are we?"

I shook my head. "No dresses. There's probably a sunrise service, and we'll eat ham for dinner and get little baskets of candy or something."

"What's a sunrise service?"

I looked at Charlie to see if she was serious. "It's a service at sunrise."

"I figured that much," she said. "But what makes than an Easter thing?"

I tried not to let my amazement show. "I think it's because the people went to Jesus' tomb at sunrise and found He was gone."

Charlie busied herself peeling bark off her dead limb. "Where'd He go?"

"He didn't go anywhere," I explained, wondering where she had been all her life. "He came back to life."

She nodded her head like she understood, but she was frowning. "How does someone come back to life?"

"Well, Jesus is God. He can do anything He wants."

Charlie held out a piece of bark she'd stripped from her branch. "Here's our bark from a dead tree." She was quiet a minute. Then she said, "I don't know much about religious stuff. I don't think I've ever been in a church in my life."

No kidding, I thought, but I didn't say anything.

Cissy and Leigh were struggling with the wastebasket, half full of water. It had been completely full before they tried walking with it. I looked at the puddles they had made as they sloshed.

"There's our mud," I said.

The New Jersey crew stirred one of the puddles with a stick until they had a blob of mud. One of them grabbed a leaf and scooped up some of the mud. She placed another leaf on top.

"I'll carry this," she said. "We can put most of the stuff back in the basket with the water, but not this."

I looked at Cissy and Leigh. "No offense, but I don't think we need that much water."

They promptly dumped out almost all of it, splashing us and washing our acorn into the stream in the process.

We all laughed, rescued the acorn, and continued our search. We found most of the things on the list, even a good skipping stone. Finally the only things we were missing were a footprint, an insect, briars, and a caterpillar.

"How in the world do we take a footprint back?" asked Charlie as she stomped her sneaker in the dirt. She lifted her foot and pointed to the print. "How do we get it up?"

We stood in a little circle, looking at the ground, thinking.

"Wait!" I had an idea. "I know what to do!"

I turned and ran back to Ponderosa again. I pulled my suitcase from under my bunk and rummaged in it until I found my sketch pad. I ripped out a page and threw the pad back in the suitcase.

As I ran out the door, I wondered where Dorian and Tracy had gone. With any luck, Dorian was calling a cab to send Tracy to her grandmother.

I was panting when I found the girls.

"Here, Charlie, stomp on this." I dropped the sheet of paper to the ground. Charlie ground her foot in the dirt, then very carefully placed it on the paper. She stood on one leg, bouncing slightly to try for more weight. When she stepped back, there was a very clear print.

We cheered, and I got elected to carry the print.

"Look! Over here!" Cissy pointed to a leaf. We gathered around, and there was an inchworm hunching his slow way across the leaf.

"I doubt this is really a caterpillar," Cissy said, "but we might not find anything better. Maybe we can talk Miss Martha into counting him as both an insect and a caterpillar."

"I doubt it," I said. "She's pretty tough. She teaches junior high the rest of the year."

Gently Cissy picked the leaf and placed it and the inchworm in our wastebasket.

"It's a good thing we dumped out most of the water, or he might drown," said Leigh. "Though the list doesn't say our caterpillar has to be alive, does it?"

In the distance the camp bell rang.

"Come on! We've got to get back," I yelled. "I know where there are some briars we can grab on our way."

We started running back to the playing field and Miss Martha.

"Shortcut!" I called. "Follow me."

We swerved off the path and into the woods, tromping through the underbrush. We came to a downed tree and climbed over it. Cissy and Leigh wanted to stay and walk on it as though it were a tilted balance beam.

"Another time," I called.

I plowed on, the others right behind me.

Suddenly a sharp pain pricked my leg, then another and another.

I looked down, expecting to see briars and thinking we wouldn't have to get them at that place near the playing field after all. Instead I saw small yellow and black insects rising out of the ground.

Charlie screamed in my ear. "Bees! Bees! She stepped on a nest of bees!"

We all turned and ran, screaming and swatting the air. The angry buzz of the bees filled my ears and scared me to death. I was, after all, the first to meet them and the last in line as we ran.

I waved the footprint madly about, but even so I got bitten. Or maybe that's why I got bitten.

"Stop waving that thing!" Charlie yelled. "You're just making them madder!"

I stopped swinging and wrapped the paper around my face and head. I jumped a mile when I felt a sharp prick right through my shorts and knew sitting would be uncomfortable for the next few days. The pain in my arms and legs was intense.

"What a stupid thing to do, Shannon!" Charlie had her arms over her head. "Ouch! Ouch! Why didn't you watch where you were going?"

I was unnerved by the nastiness in her voice. Did she think I had done it on purpose?

We raced out of the woods, the bees still attacking. Miss Martha, Dorian, and the other counselors came running, but it was the can of bug killer someone sprayed that finally sent the bees back into the woods. We were taken to the nurse's office, moaning and crying.

I hurt in several places—my legs, my bottom, my head, my ear, my arms. I had the honor of having the most stings.

Gail Macklinburg, our Sunday school teacher back home in East Edge, is the camp nurse at Harmony Hill. She's one of my favorite people in the whole world, and was I glad she was there. She took those little vials of stuff that you rub on bee stings, and in a short time, we all felt better. She made up several ice packs and handed them around.

At one point in the chaos of getting treated, I stood near Charlie.

"Get away from me, girl," she said sharply. "I don't want you near me." Her dark eyes flashed and her hair, loosened from its restraining barrettes as we ran, stuck out wildly. She looked scary.

I don't do well when people are nasty to me. I'd

never be deliberately unkind to anyone, and I can't understand why anyone else would either.

"And don't look at me like that!" she ordered. "I hate sad eyes!" She turned her back.

Gail walked up and put her arm across my shoulders. I think she'd heard Charlie and was trying to help me feel better. After all that had happened that day, I felt tears spring to my eyes at her kindness. I blinked them away.

"Sit down, Shannon," Gail said. She separated the strands of my hair, which was brown and slightly ratty with the grown-out home permanent Mom had given me at the beginning of summer.

"Right here," I said, pointing to the sorest part of my scalp.

Gail nodded and rubbed in the medicine. The pain lessened.

"Here," she said. "Keep this ice pack on your head until the ice is completely melted. I don't expect any problem except swelling, and the ice will help prevent that. I want you to come see me before you go to bed tonight and tomorrow morning as soon as you're dressed."

I nodded absently, my eyes following Charlie as she left the nurse's office with the other girls.

"Don't let her upset you," Gail said. "It's her

sharp tongue that's out of line." She hugged me.

I nodded and felt like crying again. I wanted Redwood cabin and my friends so much I ached. Then again, maybe it was just the bees.

God, I wondered as I walked to the dining room all by myself, *what's going on? Why is the week I had been looking forward to so much starting out so badly?*

In the dining room each cabin sat at its own table, the counselor at the head. When I sat next to Dorian, Charlie sat at the other end, as far from me as she could get. Tracy sat across the table from me and laughed at the ice pack I held to my head.

"I knew the woods were dangerous," she said, looking very satisfied with herself.

I wondered how she'd like the melted water from my ice pack down her neck.

Cissy and Leigh held ice packs to their arms. They had some ugly welts, but they were feeling proud because they hadn't dropped the basket of items for the scavenger hunt.

"The others didn't drop the mud, either," Cissy told me. "Of course, they hardly got bitten, but they did run just as fast as we did. We turned everything in to Miss Martha. She said we were the first cabin back, and we had everything but briars, an insect, and a footprint."

"I have the footprint," I said, excited. Maybe the day wasn't a complete loss after all. I reached in my pocket and pulled out the dirty and torn paper that had protected my face and head from more stings.

Cissy and Leigh sort of bounced in their seats. I don't know why I'd ever thought they were mousy.

"We told Miss Martha you'd have it. She said you should turn it in after dinner and it would still count."

"It seems to me that you had an insect, too," said Dorian. "In fact, you had several. And they all went buzz-zz."

Maybe that Friday night pizza could be ours after all!

After dinner we had some free time before the evening meeting. I sat on the steps of Ponderosa with my ice pack on my ear and watched some of the girls play softball. Charlie had found someone else to play tetherball with. I think she was taking out her anger on the ball. She socked it and smacked it and punched it with such fierce energy that the other girl never had a chance.

How could a bunch of bees and I make her that angry?

Cissy and Leigh sat with me for a while, and I learned that they were cousins who lived near Bethlehem, Pennsylvania. They had never been away from home before, and they had been scared to death today when their mothers drove away. Their moms had been scared too.

"I think they were crying when they drove off," said Leigh. "They've never been away from us before." She grinned. "I bet they cry themselves to sleep tonight."

"And my dad will say, 'Cheez, Louise, she's only gone for one week!' " said Cissy. "My dad always says, 'Cheez, Louise.' "

"They'll survive," said Leigh. "It'll be good for them."

Cissy shook her ice pack, and the melted water sloshed. "I think we'll have more fun than they will. I'm going to get more ice." She stood up.

"Me, too," said Leigh quickly.

I watched them run to Gail's office and had to smile. They would have fun as long as they were never separated, and even then there would be times when they were homesick. I'd seen enough first-time campers through the years to know that. I'd probably wake up some night and hear them crying into their pillows.

The girls from New Jersey, their bites hardly noticeable, sat and talked with me too. They were all in the same Sunday school class, and this was their first time at Harmony Hill. But homesickness wouldn't be a problem for them. They'd been going to camp together since they were eight years old.

"We like to try a new camp each year," said Nicole, the talker of the group. "It keeps us from getting bored."

"Really?" I said. "I love coming back to the same place every year. It makes me feel like this is my camp, you know?"

During all this socializing, Tracy lay on her bed in the cabin, making it quite clear what she thought of Harmony Hill and all of us. I almost felt sorry for her.

When the bell rang for us to go to the meeting, I wandered over to the meeting room with the New Jersey girls. We had just taken our seats beside Dorian when my ice pack sprang a leak. I jumped and shrieked as the cold water ran down my back, soaking me thoroughly.

After everyone finished laughing at me, Dorian said, "Go on back to the cabin, Shannon, and get a dry shirt."

"I'll save your seat," said Nicole from New Jersey.

I ran across the field and up the steps of Ponderosa, threw the door open, and raced into the room.

I screeched to a stop at the sight of Charlie rummaging through my suitcase.

Charlie's head jerked in my direction. She looked frightened until she saw it was only me.

"What do you want?" she asked, the chill in her voice enough to make it snow.

"Better yet," I said, "what do you want?"

She followed my gaze to the suitcase. "In here? I'm looking for my sweater."

"In my suitcase?"

"Your suitcase?" Charlie looked at the thing like it had just turned into a snake about to strike. "This isn't yours, it's mine. They said it was navy blue."

"Well, it is navy blue, so they're right there, but it most certainly is mine." I reached in, churned the clothes a bit more, and pulled out a navy sweatshirt. I held it up and there was "SHANNON" in neat red stitches with little red flowers and winding green vines hanging all over the word. "My grandmother did this for me," I said.

I pulled my wet shirt off and pulled the sweatshirt on. As I did so, Charlie reached under the bed and pulled out another navy blue suitcase. It looked nothing like mine. She stared at it a minute, then shoved it back under the bunk, stood, and walked out without a word.

"You forgot your sweater," I called after her.

When I got back to the meeting, Charlie was sitting there, eyes straight ahead. She refused to acknowledge me even when I had to climb over her to get to my seat.

I don't think she or Tracy laughed the whole evening, and there was lots to laugh at. I really felt I'd come home when we sang the "Prune Song":

No matter how old a prune may be
He's always getting wrinkles.
A baby prune is like his dad
But he's not wrinkled quite so bad.
We have wrinkles on our face;
A prune has wrinkles everyplace.
(Same song, second verse;
A little bit louder and a whole lot worse.)

When we got back to the cabin, I was feeling a warm glow in spite of certain people. It was the last week of summer vacation, and I was going to have a good time!

I had stopped after the meeting and gotten a new ice pack from Gail. I pulled out my sketch pad, climbed up to my bunk, and balanced my ice pack on my leg bites. I leaned back against the wall and doodled for a while. I drew the big bell that tells everyone at Harmony Hill when it's time to go somewhere different, and I drew our inchworm wriggling his way across the leaf.

When I showed Cissy and Leigh, they insisted we hang the pictures up for everyone to enjoy. Usually I'm happy to have my stuff where people can see it, but not here in Ponderosa. I was too afraid of snide remarks. I just folded the pad shut and stuffed everything into my suitcase.

After cabin devotions, we lay in the dark, waiting for sleep. I listened with interest for homesick crying, but I didn't hear any. But maybe I fell asleep before the tears had time to start.

It was the middle of the night when I rolled over too quickly in my sleep and my bee stings complained. I also landed on my ice pack, now a water pack.

I lay there half awake, aware enough to know that I needed to get off that side of my body and off the pack before it burst under my weight. All I lacked was the energy.

"Move, kid," I told myself and mentally shook my head in response. Finally I rolled over, congratulated myself on being so smart, and snuggled down to sleep.

I wasn't happy when I realized I needed to visit the washhouse before sleep would return. I told my bladder to stop hurting, but it didn't. I sighed mightily, threw my sleeping bag aside, and slid over the edge of the bed. Just as my feet touched the floor, I heard something scrape in the dark. A quick intake of breath followed the noise, then a rush of movement and the creak of a bunk.

Someone had bumped into a suitcase or something on the floor—someone moving quietly, too quietly—someone trying to get back to bed before I saw her.

"Who's there?" I whispered.

No one answered.

I listened for more noise, for some natural activity from someone awake like I was. I'd heard lots of girls move around a cabin in the night, and none of them had been as sneaky as this.

I realized that I was listening so hard that I had my eyes squeezed shut. I opened them cautiously and looked around. The interior of the cabin was deep in shadows from the light that burned at the edge of the field and shone weakly through the screening. I couldn't see much.

I reached for my flashlight and flicked it on. Accidentally the beam fell right across Charlie's face as she lay in the bottom bunk half in and half out of her sleeping bag.

She threw an arm over her eyes and yelped.

"Sorry," I mumbled, quickly moving the light.

"It's you," she hissed. "I might have known!" She turned away.

I moved quickly to the door and across the field. I always get the heebie-jeebies going to the washhouse alone in the middle of the night. The woods look so black and spooky.

Mom's right. I watch too much TV for someone with my sensitive imagination.

When I got back to the cabin, I stood in the doorway a minute and listened. The feeling of someone sharing the darkness, waiting, sneaking, was gone. I climbed up into bed and fell asleep.

The bell clanged an hour earlier than usual for

a Sunday morning at camp.

"Happy Easter, girls," Dorian greeted us. "Up you go. The sunrise service begins in twenty minutes."

As soon as I was dressed, I raced to Gail's office. The swelling on most of the bites was gone, but the ones on my head and ear itched like a mosquito had given them instead of a bee.

"Sit," Gail said. Even at six-thirty in the morning she looked great. She had on jeans, a rosy shirt, and a white sweater. Her hair is the same color as mine, but hers looks good. She wears it long and pulled back with combs or barrettes. I think my friend Dee over in Redwood is trying to grow her hair like Gail's, but so far Dee hasn't succeeded.

I could hear the girls singing at morning line-up.

Good morning, Lord; it's a brand new day.
Good morning, Lord; be with us we pray.
Help us to know, help us to grow,
Help us to understand that You love us so.
Good morning, Lord; it's a brand new day.

"That sounds pretty," I said, looking out the window at the girls, lined up by cabin. I saw everyone but Tracy bow her head and knew Mrs.

A. was praying. Then they began singing again, clapping with the music.

Rise and shine and give God the glory, glory.
Rise and shine and give God the glory, glory.
Rise and shine and give God the glory, glory,
Children of the Lord.

"Come here, kiddo," Gail said.

She checked my bites, put some medicine on the itchy ones, and gave me another ice pack.

"This should be your last one," she said. "You're just about healed."

We walked outside together. The morning was soft and cool. I had on my "SHANNON" sweatshirt, but I knew I'd be taking it off in a pretty short time as the sun got hotter. The humidity already made the trees across the parking lot look fuzzy.

We walked to the rows of benches at the edge of the field where morning Bible time was held. All the seats were filled, and a number of girls sat on the ground. Usually when everyone got together at one time, it was in the meeting room. But, as Dorian said, "You can't have a sunrise service inside."

Gail held up a finger. "Wait here for me," she whispered. She hurried back to her office and reappeared with two folding chairs. We sat together, a back row of two.

We were all singing when Dorian and Leigh got up and left their seats, climbing over the Ponderosa girls to get out of their row. Leigh was crying, and Dorian had her arm around her shoulders. When they got to us, Gail stood up.

"Can I help?" she asked softly. "Don't you feel well, Leigh?"

"It's not my bites, Miss Gail," she snuffled. "It's my watch."

Gail looked blank, which was how I felt. "Your watch?"

Dorian took over. "Leigh was given a watch last week for her birthday. It was a gift from her mom and dad. They told her she shouldn't bring it to camp, but she brought it anyway."

Here Leigh gave a great sniff.

"She's sure she put it on the floor beside her bunk last night before she went to the washhouse at bedtime," continued Dorian. "She put it on top of her Bible. She remembers looking at it with her flashlight just before she went to sleep."

"And this morning it was gone!" wailed Leigh. "Cissy and I looked and looked, but it's gone! Someone took my watch!"

"There was someone sneaking around the cabin last night," I said. I was in The Main Office for the second time in two days. All those years I had come to Harmony Hill and had never even seen the room, and now here I was again. Some privileges I could happily live without.

Mrs. A., Dorian, and Leigh were there, too. Cissy wanted to come, but Dorian asked her to stay with Gail. There was only so much room in The Main Office.

I was telling my story for Mrs. A.

"You're certain there was someone walking around inside Ponderosa?" Mrs. A. asked. "You didn't dream it or anything?"

"I'm certain. Whoever it was kicked something,

then dived back in bed before I saw her. I said, 'Who's there?' but no one answered. If someone had just come back from the washhouse, she would have answered me, wouldn't she?"

"And you're sure you don't know who it was?" Mrs. A. looked so concerned. Trouble like this must make her feel terrible.

"I'm sure."

While I was sure I didn't know who was moving around in the dark, I just kept seeing Charlie in my suitcase earlier in the evening. Had something of mine been taken and I didn't even know?

I thought back. Charlie had definitely been rooting in my things, but she had left the cabin with empty hands. I replayed the scene over and over, and Charlie always came up clean.

The question was what would have happened if I hadn't returned? Or had she honestly thought she was in her case? But how could you not know your own suitcase? And just because she was in my suitcase, did that mean she was the one who took Leigh's watch?

Mrs. A. sighed. "Thank you, girls," she said. "You can go. Breakfast is just being served."

I hesitated a minute before leaving. Maybe I should say something about Charlie. But as far as I

51

knew, she hadn't done anything wrong. And she'd just say she was in the wrong case by accident and get madder than ever at me.

I followed Leigh and Dorian to the dining room without speaking. What was there to say?

Cissy and I put Leigh between us at the table and tried to comfort her. Her eyes were red from crying. The New Jersey girls were extra nice to her, too. Charlie and Tracy made believe they didn't even see her. Of course, they made believe they didn't see any of us.

After breakfast everyone returned to the cabins and cleaned up for inspection. Points toward the Friday pizza are won and lost at inspection. We all made our beds and swept the floor and emptied the trash.

We were almost finished when Mrs. A. knocked on our door.

"May I come in?" she asked. "I want to talk with you all for a minute before you go to your first session. Why don't you sit on your beds and get comfortable?"

I climbed up on mine and sat cross-legged while Mrs. A. sat on the edge of Dorian's bed.

"I'm sure you are all aware that something very serious has happened in Ponderosa," Mrs. A. began.

"Sometime last night, Leigh's watch was taken. Girls, theft is wrong."

She paused and looked at each of us, one by one.

"If you have taken the watch and you return it immediately, nothing will happen. I urge you to give it back. However, if you don't return Leigh's property, we will have an investigation." She stood up. "Think about that, please. Now let's get to first session."

As I walked out the door, I thought the chances of the watch appearing on its own were very slim.

Mornings at Harmony Hill are divided into three parts. Every girl gets to choose two activities she wants, and the third part is the morning Bible time. I love making things, so I chose the craft shop for my first activity.

I decided to make a little wreath for my Christmas gift for Charlie and another one for Mom. They were easy to make. I selected a small wreath-shaped Styrofoam form and little pieces of material in several patterns and colors. I put the slightly dull point of a regular yellow pencil in the middle of the two-inch material squares and pushed the pencil into the Styrofoam. When I pulled it back, the material stayed. Lots and lots of little squares placed close together made a pretty, colorful gift.

I made Mom's wreath in pinks and blues to match her bedroom, and I made Charlie's in pinks and purples to match mine. That way, if she didn't like it, I could use it.

For second session I chose fishing. I have memories of my father taking me fishing at the stocked pond at Hibernia Park when I was real little. We used to laugh and have wonderful fun, and I always caught lots of fish. When we got home, Dad would clean them, Mom would cook them, and we'd have a party to celebrate my skill as a fisherman.

One time Mom hung streamers from the light over the table and draped them all over my chair.

"It's a good thing you caught these fish," she said. "I was ready for a party!"

Another time she made me a crown with lots of sparklies on it. It read "The Fishing Princess." She hung a towel from my shoulders like a train, and Dad got down on his knees, bowed to me, and put a pull tab from a soda can on my finger.

"This is the magic princess ring," he said. "If you wear it, you'll always be happy, and you'll always catch the biggest fish in the pond."

When I fish here at Harmony Hill, I remember those times. I pretend Dad's still in my life, even though I haven't seen him since he left us. And I try not to cry.

I could have used his magic soda tab ring this morning; I didn't even get a bite.

French Creek runs through Harmony Hill, and there's a small dam just beside the dining hall. A concrete bridge runs above the dam, and we fish from it. The creek is pretty shallow most places, and the fish like the deep area at the foot of the dam.

I've always wanted to fish from Campfire Island, a small island in the middle of the creek, but we're not allowed on the island except for the closing campfire. The only way to get there is by a narrow wooden bridge that we cross one at a time on Friday night.

The campfire program starts when all the older campers gather on shore after dark and sing, their flashlights shining up on their faces. It's spooky and special at the same time. Then one by one we walk across, singing as we go. Gradually the music moves from the shore to the island as more and more of us cross. Then we walk to the already blazing campfire.

After the campfire program is over, we sing on

the island's shore, recross the bridge one by one, and bring the music back to Harmony Hill. As we are crossing the creek, someone is dousing the campfire. By the time we're all over, the fire is gone. We sing one last song, Mrs. A. prays, and we all turn off our flashlights and return to our cabins in silence. I love it!

The reason I want to fish on Campfire Island is because at the one end there's a protected eddy. I'm convinced that Bubba, a big old grandfather catfish, lives there, but I'll probably never get a chance to prove it. I put my fishing pole away carefully because Dad had given it to me. It was in pretty bad shape, but I hated to get a new one. As long as I could hold on to this one, I held on to a bit of Dad. I sighed and went to Bible time.

Since today was Easter, Miss Evie talked about God's love and us. Miss Evie has been teaching Bible at Harmony Hill ever since I've been coming.

"People failed Jesus when He was arrested," she said. "The disciples ran. Peter lied about knowing Him. We think they were foolish and should have known better." She shrugged. "They didn't. Today some of us have been hurt by people who have failed us. We think these people should have known better too."

I thought of Dad. I knew about people letting you down, and I did think he should have known better.

"But God loves those who fail and those who are hurt by the failure," Miss Evie continued. "When Jesus rose on Easter, He proved how strong God is—strong enough to love us always, even when people fail."

At lunch, I learned that I had predicted correctly. First we had ham, and then we all got little paper baskets filled with Hershey's kisses and M & M's and marshmallow chickies.

Miss Martha, the games director, got the older cabins together outside after lunch while the little kids took their rests. She had each cabin divide into two groups. Then she gave each group a pile of newspapers, a couple of paper plates, and tape.

"Each group is going to make an Easter outfit for one girl," she told us. Her bellowing voice was good for giving directions. "Pick one person to be the model, and then the rest of you dress her. A panel of judges—Miss Evie, Mrs. A., and I—will judge the best costume, and every member of the winning team will get a chocolate Easter bunny."

I love chocolate, but I didn't have much hope for my team. Tracy sat on the ground and obviously

57

wasn't planning to help. Charlie hadn't shown any team spirit yet, and I wasn't expecting a sudden burst now. Leigh was still sniffing, and Cissy was always watching her and patting her hand.

"Come on, Leigh," I said. "You be our model." Maybe that would cheer her up. "Don't cry or you'll wrinkle the outfit."

Leigh actually grinned. It was only for a minute, but it was something.

I like competitions in which you get to be creative more than contests where you play games. I'd never made a costume of newspapers before, but it sounded like fun. I pulled off pages of newspaper and taped them to Leigh's shoulders, then taped them together down her sides. Instant blouse.

Cissy helped me wrap and tape newspapers around Leigh's arms and legs, and suddenly she had sleeves and leggings. I took pages and pages of paper and pleated them, and Cissy and I taped them on Leigh to make a skirt.

I tore one page into little squares and put the squares together. Then I stuck my finger into the middle of the squares and pushed, making the middle collapse and the sides come up. I bent and folded and twisted the squares until they looked like petals on a flower, which I taped to Leigh's "blouse" like an Easter corsage.

Cissy and I stepped back.

"Turn around," Cissy ordered our model.

Leigh, her eyes shining with fun for the first time today, spun around. One of her leggings promptly fell down.

"Take it easy!" yelled Cissy, and we taped her back together.

I tore off a couple of strips of paper, twisted them tightly, and bent them into circles. I taped the circles together, then taped them to Leigh's ears.

"Earrings," I explained. I made another circle and taped it around her wrist for a bracelet.

"I need an Easter bonnet," said Leigh.

I reached for the newspaper.

"Here," said Charlie. "I already made it."

She held out a paper plate piled high with paper flowers and feathers. Paper streamers dangled down the back.

"Charlie! That's wonderful!" I was amazed at how clever the hat was, but I was far more amazed that grumpy Charlie was participating in the fun. "Put it on her!"

Charlie set the bonnet on Leigh's head. She took two strips of newspaper that hung over the sides of the hat and taped them together under

Leigh's chin. Then she stepped back proudly.

Tracy picked herself lazily up from the ground and walked slowly around Leigh.

"Not too bad," she said. "I wouldn't have thought you could be that clever. Just one thing. I think it needs a V neck."

Quick as a flash she stepped up to Leigh, took hold of the newspaper blouse at the neck, and tore it right down the middle.

While we stared, too stunned to react, she stepped calmly back.

"Much better," she said. "But that hat . . ." She shook her head in mock disgust.

This time Charlie moved faster than Tracy, stepping between Tracy's outstretched arm and Leigh.

"Don't even think of touching that hat," Charlie hissed. "I'm not as nice as most of the people here, and I'll break your head."

We managed to put a new blouse on Leigh and tape her skirt back in place before the judging. I was flabbergasted when we won the chocolate rabbits. Cheering all the way, we took them back to Ponderosa, split them in half and shared them with the New Jersey girls. They had made Nicole their model and wrapped her up like a mummy. The judges hadn't been impressed.

Leigh hung her hat over the end of her bunk, but it didn't want to stay. Dorian wasn't there, so I whipped out my stapler and stapled the hat to the bedpost.

"Uh-oh," said Charlie. "I'm telling. Little Miss Goody-Goody isn't so good after all."

Tracy wasn't with us for our little rabbit picnic.

Unfortunately for her, Dorian had seen her rip Leigh's costume, and now she was visiting Mrs. A.

We lay on our bunks, enjoying the chocolate and talking about Tracy.

"Why is she so mean?" asked Leigh. "I can't understand it."

"She's unhappy," said Charlie.

"So am I," said Leigh. "I lost my birthday watch. But I'm not ruining people's things."

"You're not unhappy enough," Charlie said.

"You mean because her mother and father don't seem to like her?" I asked.

"Precisely," answered Charlie.

"Well, my father doesn't seem to like me either," I said, "but I don't tear other people's things apart."

"Your father doesn't like you?" said Charlie in disbelief. "You're just trying to make me feel better."

She placed her feet on the bottom of my mattress and gave me a little bounce.

I giggled.

"Everybody likes you," she said, bouncing me harder. "Your father probably likes you best of all."

"Don't I wish," I said, holding on to the sides of my bed so I wouldn't tumble off. I laughed as Charlie bounced me faster and faster. I knew she was trying to scare me, but I wouldn't give in. Why was it that everything she did took on an edge of anger?

Nicole placed her feet on the bottom of the mattress above her and started to bounce Judy, who started to whoop. Cissy tried to bounce Leigh, but her feet wouldn't reach high enough for her to do more than touch the mattress with her toes.

Suddenly Charlie got carried away with her bouncing and gave me a mighty push. I flew out of the bed, sailed through the air, and hit the floor with a terrible crash.

For a moment no one moved, including me. When I finally got my breath back, I started to laugh. I laughed so hard that I cried. Cissy, Leigh, and Nicole thought I was hurt and rushed to help me.

I noticed that Charlie stayed on her bed.

"She's laughing," said Cissy in disbelief. "She's laughing!"

"Are you sure you're not hurt?" asked Leigh. "You ought to be dead!"

I waved a hand to show I was fine and pulled myself to my feet. I lurched to my bed, grabbed my pillow, and walloped Charlie with it.

She froze in surprise for just an instant, then

grabbed her pillow and struck back hard. In no time all of us were having the best pillow fight I'd ever seen. I ended up laughing so hard I couldn't even swing.

Dorian, who had returned without our noticing, had to blow her whistle three times before we even heard her. Then she acted like she was mad because the cabin was a mess. We straightened it up and went swimming for the rest of the afternoon.

Tracy finally appeared at the pool, looking ready to bite anyone who talked to her. Of course, Charlie went right over.

"I'm surprised you're still here," Charlie said. "I thought they'd send you home."

"They can't send me home," Tracy said. "No one's there. Mom and Horrible Harry are somewhere in the middle of the Pacific Ocean on a cruise."

"Who's Horrible Harry?" I asked.

"My mother's new husband."

"Is he really horrible?" My mother would have said I should mind my own business, but I wanted to know.

"You saw him," Tracy said.

"The bored guy in the doorway?"

She nodded. "I hate him."

Ever-kind Charlie said softly, "I wonder how he feels about you?"

Monday was Valentine's Day. I dressed at top speed, then pulled my construction paper, scissors, and tape from my suitcase. I cut and bent and taped until I had a huge red paper chain, which I draped around the door. I made another and hung it from my bunk.

"What are you doing?" asked Charlie when she returned from the washhouse. She stared at my decorations without pleasure.

"Decorating for Valentine's Day," I said. "Just my bed."

"Well, your bed is my bed, and it looks dumb. Take it down."

"No, no!" said Cissy and Leigh. "Leave it alone. It's great! Can we make some?"

They started cutting and taping while Charlie flopped on her bed in a sulk.

During first session I finished Charlie's Christmas present in the craft shop, and during second I caught a fish from the dam. I looked at the area off Campfire Island where Bubba lived.

"Can I fish over there some afternoon?" I asked the counselor in charge.

"Not from the island," I was told. "It's strictly off limits till Friday night. Besides, a skunk is living there now, and you don't want to meet him."

I certainly didn't.

"But if you've passed your swimming test, you can take a rowboat out and fish from that."

All right! Look out, Bubba. Here I come!

When I went to Bible time, I was in a great mood.

"When things happen that we don't understand, God is still in control," Miss Evie reminded us. "And we know we can trust Him to control wisely because He loves us. Today is Valentine's Day, and when you make your valentines, remember God's love for you."

Do You love me as much as my father did? I wondered quietly. *Will You leave me the way he did? But You can't leave me and still be God, can You?*

After lunch we went back to Ponderosa and made valentines for each other. I let people use my glitter and glue, and by the time we finished, it looked like a silver and gold snowfall had occurred.

"Just remember that this stuff all has to be swept out by inspection tomorrow morning," Dorian reminded us. "There's no way we'll get pizza Friday night if it isn't."

"Don't worry," Charlie said. "Miss Sparkle will sweep it all up." She looked at me, and I wondered why she had to mock all the time.

I grabbed my swimsuit and pulled it on. I wasn't going to stay here with Charlie. She drove me crazy.

I grabbed my towel from the clothesline and stalked to the pool. If I kept busy, I wouldn't give in to the temptation to go to the craft shop and pull all the little material squares out of her wreath.

It wasn't long before New Jersey Nicole and Judy joined me. They looked distracted.

"What's wrong?" I asked.

They looked at each other, then back at me.

"Our towels are gone," Nicole said.

Judy nodded. "We hung them on the line yesterday, but they aren't there now. They're gone."

We looked at each other, all thinking the same thing, but not willing to say it.

Finally I forced myself to speak. "You think they've been stolen like Leigh's watch?"

On the breakfast table Tuesday were little turkeys with fold-out puffy tummies. Thanksgiving Day! I smiled and hoped that we would have turkey with stuffing and pumpkin pie for dinner.

I love turkey, but we never have it at home anymore. Mom says that the two of us would be eating turkey for a month if she got one. I'm sure she's right, but I'd still like to have it more often than on the real Thanksgiving and Christmas at Grandmom's.

I sat across the table from Tracy and watched her unhappy face. I also listened while she ignored Charlie's request for the pancakes. I picked up the plate and passed it. Charlie didn't bother to say thank you.

Watching Tracy reminded me that I had drawn her name for Birthday Day. I didn't want to make a gift for her. She wasn't worth it. I decided I'd buy her a candy bar, preferably the kind she liked least.

During cabin cleanup I spent a long time sweeping up the glitter from yesterday's cutting and pasting, but I didn't mind. The valentines had been great, especially the ones Charlie made. We had them taped to our bunks. I hoped the inspection team didn't think that was messy. I still wanted that pizza.

My wreath for Mom was almost done, and I'd have time to make another project before the week was over. I looked at all the things available just before I left the craft shop at the end of first session, but nothing looked very exciting.

It was time for second session, and I ran back to Ponderosa for my fishing pole. This morning I'd relax with my rod at the dam, but in the afternoon I was going to go for Bubba in a rowboat. A couple of my East Edge friends were coming too. Cammi and Dee didn't particularly like to fish, but they said they'd row for the fun of it.

When I reached for my pole, it wasn't where I'd left it. *Maybe it's on the other side of the bed,* I thought. I climbed across Charlie's bunk and looked on the other side. No rod.

I dropped to my knees and looked under the bed. Maybe it had slipped down and rolled under.

No rod.

I crawled around on my knees, looking under every bunk. I even looked under Dorian's bed.

No rod.

I sat back on my heels and stared at Dorian's pillow. Where was my fishing rod? What could have happened to it?

Suddenly I noticed that Dorian had a stuffed bear tucked into her sleeping bag. I leaped to my feet. Maybe someone had put my rod in my sleeping bag for a joke.

I ran to my bed and threw back the bag. Nothing.

I felt my heart pounding harder and harder. I rested my forehead on the edge of my bed. Not my fishing rod! Dad had given it to me, and I couldn't lose it!

I went outside and looked under the cabin.

"What are you doing?" It was Charlie.

"My fishing pole's missing!"

"Yeah? Surprise, surprise," she said.

"What surprise?" Tracy asked as she bent and looked under the cabin with me. I think it was the first time she had shown an interest in anything.

"Shannon's lost her fishing rod." Charlie said. She smiled, unconcerned, and Tracy smiled back. A caring pair if I ever saw one.

"I have not lost it!" I was angry that she treated my missing pole as though it weren't important. "Someone's taken it!"

Charlie shrugged. "Could be, considering. But who would want an old fishing rod?"

"Really," agreed Tracy. "At least a watch is worth taking."

I look at them both and ran to the nurse's office. I had to talk to someone who cared.

"It's gone!" I shouted as I ran into the room. "My fishing rod my father gave me is gone!"

Gail understood right away. She put her arms around me and held me.

"It'll be all right," she said softly. "It'll be all right."

I cried on her shoulder.

"Why would anyone do something so mean?" I sobbed.

Gail led me to a chair and sat me down.

"Chances are," she said as she pushed my hair out of my eyes, "that no one realized how special your rod was to you. Where did you have it?"

"Leaning against the wall beside my bed."

"Then someone took it because it was easy to get to," she said. "Whoever's taking the things in Ponderosa isn't searching for them very hard. She's taking whatever is handy—a watch on the floor, towels on the clothesline, a fishing pole resting against the wall."

"It just hurts so badly," I said.

But if I was upset, it was nothing compared to the storm Tracy kicked up when she discovered that her Disney World sweatshirt was gone.

"Who stole my shirt?" she demanded.

We were standing around in various amounts of clothing, getting ready to go swimming.

"Come on!" she demanded. "Who took it?"

She walked around the cabin, looking at everyone accusingly. I half expected her to point her finger in each face and yell, "Was it you?"

"What does it look like?" asked Dorian.

"It's white with 'Disney World' on the front. Each letter is a different color of the rainbow. You know—red, orange, yellow, green, blue, violet."

Dorian nodded.

"It has a hood lined in red. And it's almost brand new!"

"When did you get it?" I asked, nosy as always.

72

"In May. Horrible Harry took us to Florida to try and win me over. He let me take a couple of friends along, and we had a room of our own and everything."

I watched her with interest. She was actually getting excited at the memory.

"When we went somewhere, Horrible Harry would give us money and let us go off by ourselves. We were allowed to eat lunch wherever we wanted and spend the money any way we wanted. He used to give me more in one day than my mother's willing to leave me for the entire week! My sweatshirt is one of the things I bought."

She looked thoughtful for a minute. Then she laughed.

"We were supposed to eat dinner each night with Harry and Mom, but we made the first night so terrible by complaining and fighting that he gave us money to go eat dinner by ourselves too. It was like being on vacation alone, just us kids."

"Sounds to me like Harry wasn't so horrible then," I said.

Tracy's smile disappeared fast, and she looked at me with dislike. "That shows how much you know." She threw herself on her bed and refused to go swimming.

"Funny," said Charlie as she grabbed her towel to go to the pool. "Camp Harmony Hill has become Camp Catastrophe."

I didn't think it was funny at all. Before I left the cabin, I asked Tracy another question. "Where was your sweatshirt?"

"Aren't you the nosy one?" she sneered. "It was in my suitcase."

"Under your bed?"

She nodded. "Why?"

"Just curious."

Gail had said that our thief was taking things that were handy. Tracy's shirt wasn't handy. Someone had to get down on her knees, pull out a suitcase, and root through it. That made a longer time in which to chance getting caught. Our thief was getting braver.

When we woke up Wednesday, I was almost afraid to get up. What would be missing today? Who would be hurt?

I felt sad that Harmony Hill had become Camp Catastrophe. It just wasn't fair.

Late yesterday afternoon Mrs. A. had talked to each one of us separately about the thefts. I don't know how anyone else had felt, but I know I was nervous. What if she didn't believe me when I said I hadn't taken anything?

But she had been very nice to me, and I could tell she knew I wasn't the thief.

"If you see or hear anything more, Shannon, come to me immediately," she said.

I nodded. "Don't worry, I will. I want this thief

found too." And the sooner the better.

Now I stared at the ceiling a few minutes, trying to wake up. I finally rolled out, reached under my bed, and pulled out the paper chain from Valentine's Day.

"Merry Christmas, everyone," I said. "I'm not letting some thief ruin my fun for me!"

I draped the chains over the door and on my bed again. Cissy and Leigh hung theirs, too, and the New Jersey girls produced a chain where the circles alternated between red and green.

"Where'd you get that?" I asked, impressed.

"We made it yesterday afternoon in the craft shop," said Judy.

"While you were trying to get Bubba," said Nicole.

Miss Martha had taken pity on me and lent me her pole to fish in the rowboat off Campfire Island. I had spent an hour with my line in the water, and enjoyed being with Cammi and Dee, but somehow it wasn't the same without my own rod. Bubba didn't pay me a visit.

Because today was Christmas, we sang "Away in a Manger" at morning lineup instead of "Good Morning, Lord" and "Jingle Bells" instead of "Rise and Shine." It was fun singing Christmas carols when the weather was so warm that I hadn't had "SHANNON" on for two days. Maybe, I thought hopefully, the thief won't take anything on Christmas.

I was wrong. It was during cabin cleanup that our latest theft was discovered. We were all working quietly when Dorian clapped her hands for our attention.

I turned toward her and was surprised at how pale she looked.

"I think this has gone on long enough," she said. "What you are doing is wrong, very wrong! I'd appreciate it if you'd return my Bible. My parents gave it to me when I was twelve. It's very special to me because we had no money that year, and my Bible was the only gift I got."

Her eyes welled with tears, and I knew exactly how she felt.

"My fishing rod's special to me, too," I said.

"And my watch," said Leigh.

"Don't forget my sweatshirt," said Tracy.

"I wouldn't say our towels are all that special," said Nicole, shrugging her shoulders. "But they do belong to us, not to whoever you are."

We stood there for a few minutes. One of us was a thief. It seemed preposterous. Thieves didn't come to Harmony Hill.

"Well," said Charlie, snickering slightly, "come to Harmony Hill, the camp with its own criminal."

"Camp Catastrophe," said Tracy.

"Charlie! Tracy!" said Dorian as the bell rang for first session. "This is no laughing matter!"

I stopped at the nurse's office on my way to the craft shop.

"I thought you'd like to know that we've had another theft," I said to Gail.

"I heard about Tracy's shirt. Poor girl. Things haven't been easy for her lately."

"Poor girl? She's a pain in the neck!"

"Because she's sad," Gail explained.

Sometimes I wondered if maybe Gail weren't too understanding.

"I have her name for Birthday Day, and I wish I didn't," I said.

"Are you going to make her a wreath like you did for your mother and Charlie?"

"I thought I'd buy her a candy bar." I didn't mention the kind-she-liked-least part. I knew Gail wouldn't approve.

Gail thought for a moment. "Candy bars are fine for other girls to give, but you're so good at making things. I think you should make her a wreath."

"But I don't even like her."

"You don't have to like her to be nice to her."

I had to think about that idea for a while. "I wonder what colors would be good."

Gail shook her head. "I have no idea."

"Wait a minute," I said. "I think I know." I thought a bit longer. "No, I can't."

"Can't what?" said Gail.

"Tracy's shirt that was stolen had letters like a rainbow. I thought I could make a wreath like a rainbow, a clump of red material blending into a clump of orange and so on."

Gail smiled. "That's a great idea!"

"Except that the craft shop doesn't have material like that."

"No problem," said Gail. "I have today off, and I'm going shopping in just a couple of minutes. I'll stop and get material for you."

"You will?" I felt like I was going under for the third time, drowning in Gail's niceness. I sighed. "Okay, I'll do it because you asked me to. But, by the way, Tracy's not why I came. It's Dorian. Her Bible's been stolen."

Gail looked pained. "Do you have any idea who is doing this, Shannon? Any clue at all?"

"I wish I did. I want my rod back."

I went on to the craft shop and finished Mom's wreath. I told myself I was glad I was going to make one for Tracy, but I couldn't convince myself.

When the bell rang to end first session, I walked back to Ponderosa for Miss Martha's fishing rod. I climbed the steps slowly, still thinking about Tracy. Was Horrible Harry as bad as she said? How would I feel if Mom brought some man home to be my new father? I shivered at the idea.

My hand was almost on the door when I heard something scrape across the floor inside the cabin. I stopped, and instead of going inside, I moved to the side of the door and peered cautiously through the screen.

The cabin was empty except for Charlie. She was on her knees on the far side of our bed, looking at something I couldn't see. She had a funny look on her face.

Quickly she stood, pushing her suitcase back under her bed with a foot. Her hands hung at her sides, and I could see a Bible in one. The other was clenched around something.

She turned and walked quickly across the cabin and out of my line of vision. Then she swung around and started for the door.

I didn't want her to see me and think I was

spying on her (which I guess I was, though I hadn't planned it), so I hurried to the edge of the porch and jumped the rail. I pressed myself against the side of the cabin and listened as she walked slowly outside and down the steps. She went over toward the kickball game in progress at the far end of the field. There was nothing in her hands.

As soon as I thought she wouldn't see me, I raced around the cabin and up the steps. I stood where she had stood beside our bed, turned in the direction she had, and began to walk. I ended up beside Cissy and Leigh's bunk. And there on Leigh's pillow lay her watch. So that was what had been clenched in Charlie's hand. Then I went to Dorian's bed, and there lay her Bible.

Charlie. I thought I'd feel good if I caught the thief, but I just felt sad. I didn't want it to be Charlie. I didn't even want it to be Tracy. To tell the truth, I didn't want it to be anybody.

"So it must be Charlie," I told Mrs. A. and Dorian. I had found them together in The Main Office.

Mrs. A. nodded. "Thank you, Shannon," she said. "I'm going to ask you to keep this information to yourself. I want to talk with Charlie personally. After all, this is a Christian camp, and we want to help girls, not punish them."

I nodded.

I thought of Charlie a lot during morning Bible time.

"Jesus loved us so much He left heaven on that first Christmas and came to earth," said Miss Evie. "The people who met Him that night had no idea who He was or what He was going to do. They didn't even understand that the baby proved God's love for them. And for us. Because of Christmas, we know God loves us very much."

I was starting to get the idea that God's love fills in the holes left when other people—like dads—don't love us the way they ought to.

God, I want to learn to believe in Your love more and more all the time, I prayed silently.

Mrs. A. spoke with Charlie during the afternoon. When she returned to the cabin, her eyes were red from crying, and she looked awful.

"Are you all right?" asked Cissy.

"Sure," said Charlie. "Absolutely great." She threw herself stomach first on her bed and buried her face in her pillow. "Just leave me alone until Saturday when I can leave this awful place."

"Is she the thief?" Leigh asked as we walked to the pool. "Did she get caught or something?"

I shrugged my shoulders and for once kept my mouth shut. "You'd have to ask Mrs. A."

Leigh nodded her head. "She probably is."

"I don't want her to be the thief," I said.

"You don't want anyone to be the thief," Leigh said. "You're too kind."

Somehow she made kindness sound like a fatal disease.

We had our cabin Christmas party that night just before bed. Judy had drawn my name and gave me a leather key chain she'd stamped with my initials. It was just like one I'd made in the craft shop for my father three years ago.

"Thanks, Judy," I said. "I like it a lot."

Charlie sat back on her bunk, careful not to enter into the fun, careful not to smile.

"Here, Charlie," I said. "Open your gift."

She looked at the package I placed beside her with little interest.

"Come on, Charlie," said Dorian. "If you're not curious, I am."

Charlie pulled the paper away and sat, staring at the wreath.

I couldn't handle her lack of reaction. "Don't you like it?" I couldn't help asking. "Aren't the colors good?"

"Did you make it?" she asked, running her hand slowly across the fabric.

I nodded. That must be the problem. She didn't like handmade gifts.

"Like your grandmother made your sweatshirt?"

"Sort of."

She stared at the wreath some more. Then she said, so softly I barely heard her, "No one ever made me a gift before." And she lay back, hugging the wreath to her chest.

Thursday we had an old-fashioned picnic to celebrate the Fourth of July. There were hot dogs, snow cones, and popcorn to eat whenever we wanted. And there were relay races and games and lots of fun.

For one game they divided the senior camp into two groups and gave each group a five-pound block of ice.

"Whoever melts their block first wins!" shouted Miss Martha. "And you can't eat it!"

We took turns sitting or lying on our ice, thinking our body heat would melt it.

"I'll time each of us," said Leigh, waving her watch around.

She was so happy and relieved to have that

watch back. I hoped it was waterproof, because I didn't think she'd ever take it off again, not even to shower or swim.

"One minute each," she announced.

But sitting on the ice didn't do much of anything except get everyone very uncomfortable very fast.

"I'm not sitting on that," announced Tracy when it was her turn. "I'm not giving myself frostbite!"

For once we sort of agreed, especially those of us who had already had our turns.

"We could break it into pieces," said Charlie suddenly.

She seemed to be feeling much better today than she had yesterday after her interview with Mrs. A. I was glad. It seemed a terrible waste of time to spend the rest of the week lying on your bunk with your face buried in your pillow.

Charlie continued, "They said we couldn't eat it, but they didn't say anything about breaking it."

"Breaking it with what?" I asked.

"Who knows?" she said. "I gave you the idea. You figure out how to do it."

"A baseball bat?"

It was Tracy, of all people, actually making a useful suggestion.

We beat our poor ice block to pieces, and the

little chunks melted much faster than the big one would have. Score one for our team.

Next we lined up with wedges of watermelon in our hands

"Whoever spits her seeds the farthest wins!" yelled Miss Martha.

The little white seeds were no good at all, but the black seeds carried pretty well once you got the knack. As a return camper who had spit seeds other summers and who practiced at home whenever the occasion arose, I was pretty good. I won by at least two inches.

We had three-legged races, sack races, egg tosses, and wrestling matches with greased watermelons in the pool. It was great fun! But the best part of the day was coming after dark: Mission Impossible!

"Everybody must wear long sleeves and long pants," said Gail at dinner. "In fact, tuck your pants into your socks. There's poison ivy all over the place, and you need to protect yourselves."

If Mom were here, she would have added, "And don't forget the deer ticks. We don't want any cases of Lyme's disease."

At bedtime, instead of putting on pajamas, girls were dressing in dark clothing, waiting with anticipation for the bell to announce the beginning of the contest.

"The Ponderosa flag is near the French Creek Crossing," Dorian said. "Do you know where I'm talking about?"

"Where the creek gets real shallow and wide, and the water only reaches your ankles when you walk across," I said.

She nodded. "Retrieve your flag and get back here first without getting caught, and you win. Stay together as a cabin as much as you can. If you get separated, you won't know where the others on your team are or what they're doing."

I looked at our two rebels, Charlie and Tracy. Who knew what they would do?

"All the counselors and staff will be out there trying to stop you," Dorian continued. "We'll all have flashlights which we have to keep lit at all times. If we pin you in our beam, you're out of the game. Good luck!"

Suddenly the bell rang and we were off.

We dashed toward the creek just as a staff car came zipping across the field, headlights blazing. We were going to get caught in its beam before we even began!

"Behind this cabin!" I yelled and we all dived at

once, landing on top of each other. We lay there giggling until the car and its deadly headlights turned away.

Very slowly we got to our knees.

"Let's travel in the woods," suggested Charlie. "It's too open by the creek."

"If we get separated," I said, "we'll meet at the Crossing."

Everyone nodded and we ducked behind the cabins into the woods. We ran along the same path we had followed the first day on our scavenger hunt. To me we seemed as quiet as a herd of elephants, snorting, thrashing, and stomping.

Suddenly a flashlight shone on the path ahead.

"Hide!" shrieked Cissy.

As if we didn't know! We dashed behind a huge pair of mountain laurel bushes and crouched there, trying not to make any noise until the flashlight passed us. I was beside Leigh, who was trembling with nervousness and excitement.

"This is great!" she whispered in my ear.

When it was safe, we crept out of hiding. We had gone only a few feet when someone yelled, "Got you!"

We spun around, hearts in our throats, and saw a flashlight beam nailing a laughing Gail.

"I'm on your team," she said to the flashlight.

"I know," said Miss Evie. "I'm just practicing."

We got out of there fast, stumbling along until we came to a stone fence.

"Do we have to climb this?" asked Tracy unhappily.

"Yes, and hurry up!" I sputtered. "Here comes a light!"

I hit the ground on the other side first, and the whole cabin landed on top of me. It felt like more elbows and knees jabbed in my back than it was possible for nine girls to have.

"There's the creek," I hissed when we finally unpiled. "Now to the Crossing."

We moved to the edge of the woods and looked out cautiously. It was a dark night with the moon hidden by clouds, but the water tumbled white over some little rapids in front of us.

"This way," I whispered.

We snaked single file along the creek bank, looking out for flashlights. When the headlights of a camp van suddenly appeared on the road across the creek, we dived for cover. Somehow I got bumped into the creek and got wet from my feet to my waist. I hid my face in the bank until the van rumbled past.

"How long before it comes by again?" asked Nicole.

"Who knows?" I said. "There's the Crossing. Let's find that flag and get out of here!"

We looked and looked and looked. I even waded across to the other side, tripping all the way on stones I couldn't see.

"Dorian said the flag was near the Crossing, right?" Charlie asked.

I nodded. A raindrop, then two, then three, bounced on my head.

"How near is 'near the Crossing'?"

"Good question. I don't know. It's raining."

We all looked up the way you do when it starts to rain, and there was our flag, flying from a branch over our heads. I jumped for it and almost touched it, but it was Leigh who swarmed up the tree and out onto the branch to grab it. She had just dropped it to us when we heard the van returning.

"I knew it!" wailed Nicole as we threw ourselves flat—all except Leigh, who was caught on her branch.

I held my breath as the van reached us. I expected the brakes to squeal and the driver to yell, "I see you up in that tree!" But it never stopped.

We jumped to our feet, pulled Leigh down, and

headed for Ponderosa. Halfway there we dashed behind a huge rock to hide and literally ran into the girls from Redwood who were already hiding there. We all started giggling so hard I was sure we'd be caught, especially when the flashlight stopped by our rock and scanned the woods ever so slowly. We ducked our heads and held our breath. We couldn't get caught so close to success!

I was sitting with my foot bent under me, and I could feel it going to sleep while the flashlight lingered. Finally the beam moved on, but we stayed put a minute to be sure we were safe.

"Do you have your flag yet?" I whispered to Dee, who was next to me.

Her bangs were plastered to her forehead from the rain, and she looked unhappy. She shook her head. "It's supposed to be here at the rock, but we've looked and looked, and we can't find it!"

"Look up," I suggested, standing and pointing. "It worked for us."

I took a step—or tried to—and staggered out onto the path, my leg prickling and painful, just as another flashlight popped into view.

I knew I was dead meat. I couldn't move fast enough to get back behind the rock with my leg feeling all wooden and weird.

Suddenly Tracy stood up and tossed a stone into the woods near the flashlight. As the beam swung toward the noise of the falling stone, she grabbed me and yanked me down beside her. We huddled there until the danger was past.

Imagine Tracy helping someone! Imagine Tracy helping me!

When we got back to camp, we had to crouch behind Ponderosa for what seemed forever while we waited for Miss Martha and Miss Evie to stop talking by our front steps. By now it was raining steadily, though I was so wet from the creek I didn't care about the rain. What's a little more water when you're already thoroughly soaked?

Just when we began to think we'd never get a chance to get safely inside before dawn, another cabin raced around the side of the dining hall, heading for home.

Miss Martha and Miss Evie, attracted by their noise, walked in that direction, their flashlight beams cutting the darkness. Quietly, quietly we tiptoed up our steps. When we were all safely on the porch, we began to cheer. We waved our flag and jumped up and down.

We had won.

The rain fell and fell and fell. Nobody minded when we tumbled exhausted into bed and slept the night away, but dodging drops the next day was a bother. I ended up with soaked sneakers, and my ponytail kept dripping down my neck.

By afternoon the rain was almost a solid curtain of water.

"How come we can still find oxygen to breathe out there?" asked Charlie, collapsing on her bunk in a heap. "The rain's so thick that you'd think there wouldn't be room for air in the air."

With the awnings down to keep us dry, everything in the cabin was dark and depressing and damp to the touch. The single light in the center of the ceiling helped some, but I felt gloomy as I lay on my bunk. Last night's Mission Impossible fun seemed ages ago.

Charlie lay beneath me as usual, and Tracy lay in her bunk. The three of us were alone in Ponderosa. Tracy's back wasn't to us, but she was withdrawn. It was as if I'd imagined the girl who'd played Mission Impossible with us and saved me from getting caught last night.

It was Birthday Day. Rainy, dreary, weepy Birthday Day.

My birthdays used to be wonderful when Dad was home. He and Mom gave me parties and invited all my friends. Once Dad dressed as a clown and played magic tricks for us all afternoon. Another time he made a fun house for us in the cellar where we felt spaghetti in the dark and he said it was intestines.

"Shannon." It was Charlie.

"Hmmm?"

"What would you ask for if you could have anything you wanted for your birthday?"

I didn't even have to think. "I'd ask for a week at Disney World where I would buy a Disney World sweatshirt of my own. . . . But what I really want more than anything in the world is my father."

Charlie was quiet for a while. Then she said,

"You really don't see him? You weren't fooling the other day?"

"I haven't seen him for two years," I said. "He left us and went to California. He told me I wouldn't miss him, but he was wrong." I felt the familiar tears burn my eyes. "He thinks girls don't need dads."

"Parents are dumb sometimes," said Charlie.

"Tell me about it."

I knew Tracy was listening to our conversation. We lay in silence for a few minutes.

"What about your father?" I asked Charlie.

"Don't ask me," she said, her voice hard. "I've never even met the man."

"You know what?" I rolled on my stomach and looked over the edge of my bed to see Charlie, who was lying with her hands tucked behind her head. "When I talk about my father, I want to cry. When you talk about your family, you sound like you want to punch somebody."

Charlie snorted. "You're too smart."

I lay back on my pillow. "Tell me about your mother," I said.

I heard Charlie move, and I peered down at her again. She had rolled onto her side and pulled her knees up to her chest. Her arms were wrapped around her knees, and she looked little and sad.

I lay back on my pillow. Charlie, little and sad?

"My mother . . ." Charlie's voice was muffled in her pillow. She cleared her throat and started again. "My mother . . ." And she began to cry. Not little, gentle sobs like I cry when I think of Dad, but huge, loud, painful cries that shook the whole bed. She scared me to death.

"What did your mother do?" It was Tracy.

While I lay glued to my bunk, not knowing what to do, Tracy sat up and looked at Charlie. "What did she do? Marry some terrible man like my mother did?"

I peered down at Charlie. Her face was white with anger, but her eyes were filled with tears.

"I'm not allowed to live with her anymore," Charlie whispered. "She used to beat me, and she drinks a lot, but she's my mother! I know she doesn't take good care of me, but she's all I've got. I love her, and I think she loves me, but they won't let me live with her anymore."

Tracy was as floored as I was. Whatever we had expected to hear, it wasn't this. The three of us waited in the darkened cabin while the rain drip, drip, dripped, weeping with Charlie.

Finally Charlie's sobs died to a hiccup.

"See why I get mad?" she said. "It's so much

better than crying."

"I don't know," I said. "Anger tends to hurt other people. Crying helps wash away pain, at least for a while."

"Will the pain ever go away for good?" Charlie asked in a little voice.

"I don't know," I said. "I know I still hurt. But God loves me. That idea helps a lot. I know He loves me and He'll take care of me."

"If He loves you so much, why did He let your father go away?" Tracy asked, her voice hard. "Why did He let Charlie's mother become a drunk? Why did He let my mom marry Horrible Harry?"

I shook my head. "He didn't make them do those things. People just don't pay attention to Him sometimes, and they do what they want. What I mean is that He loves me always, even when I'm hurting. He'll never leave me like Dad did, because He's God and He loves me."

Tracy snorted. "Lucky you."

"He loves you, too, Tracy. You're hurting right now because things aren't the way you want, but God still loves you."

Tracy shook her head. "I don't know, Shannon. I just don't know."

We lay in silence, thinking our own thoughts.

"You know what, Shannon?" It was Charlie. She had uncurled from her tight ball and was lying on her side. "I'm living in East Edge."

"What?" I dropped from my bed and sat on Charlie's. "You've got to be kidding!"

"With a lady named Ginny Anderson."

"I know her!" I exclaimed. "She takes in foster kids all the time. She goes to my church! You'll go to my school!"

Charlie smiled lopsidedly. "I hate being a foster kid," she said sadly. "I hate it, I hate it, I hate it."

"At least you'll have someone who cares," said Tracy. And she lay down and turned away from us.

"Tracy," I said to her back, "God cares about you. He loves you."

She didn't respond.

"Remember when you found me in your suitcase?" Charlie asked after a minute.

I nodded.

"I really thought it was mine. I want you to know that. I was only at Mrs. Anderson's for two days before they brought me here. 'You have a navy blue suitcase,' they told me. But it wasn't one I'd ever seen before."

"It's okay," I said.

"I'd never seen most of the clothes in my suitcase,

either, because Mrs. Anderson bought them for me just for camp, so I really didn't know it wasn't mine. Until you pulled out that sweatshirt."

"My 'SHANNON' shirt," I said.

"When I saw that, it was like a punch in my heart. All I've ever wanted was for my mother to love me, and she never has. Or at least she's never shown it. That sweatshirt was like a sign of a loving family, and it got me upset. And when I'm upset, I'm . . . bad."

"Mouthy," I said.

"Critical," she said.

"Nasty," said Tracy without turning around.

At that moment Cissy and Leigh burst through the door. Their raincoats were dripping, and they shook themselves off like puppies.

"Look!" Cissy said. She pulled a sun-catcher from under her coat. It was a clown with lots of different colors in his costume and a red wig. "He'll look beautiful when he hangs in the window over the kitchen sink. Mom will love him." She grinned. "Of course she'd love him even if he was ugly, because I made it."

Charlie and I looked at each other, and she gave me a sad smile.

"We finally finished our birthday gifts," Leigh

said. She placed a wrapped gift on her pillow. "No peeking, Shannon," she said.

Of course I immediately went and looked.

"Does it look like tickets to Disney World?" asked Charlie.

I turned to grin at her and saw Tracy's back.

"I've got to go to the craft shop for a few minutes," I said. "I've still got some work to do on a rainbow."

There's something very cozy about cuddling
warm and dry in your sleeping bag in the darkness
while rain falls on the cabin roof. I snuggled
down, toasty with memories of Ponderosa's
birthday party.

Leigh had given me a sun-catcher just like the
one Cissy made for her mom. I planned to hang it
in my bedroom window and remember this week
whenever I looked at it.

It was strange to think about. Last Saturday I
was so upset about not being in Redwood. Now I
was so glad I had been put in Ponderosa.

I had given Tracy her gift last. She sat on her
bed the whole party, not participating, sort of lost
in the shadows. She did give Cissy a gift of two

Snickers bars—Cissy's favorite candy—and she'd seemed pleased when Cissy promptly ate one. But that was it.

I pulled my present out and put in on Tracy's bed. It was obvious from its shape what it was.

"I made this especially for you," I said. "I picked the colors because they're the ones in your Disney World sweatshirt."

Tracy slid forward and touched the gift hesitantly. I watched her face. For some reason it was important to me that she like what I had done.

Slowly she took off the paper until a rainbow colored wreath was revealed. She looked at it, then at me. She ran her fingers over the red, orange, yellow, green, blue, and violet material scraps.

"Where did you get these colors?" she asked. "I didn't see them in the craft shop."

"I had Gail buy them for me on her day off."

"Gail the nurse?"

I nodded again. "We knew you were unhappy, and we wanted to do something special for you."

"After the way I acted?"

I shrugged. "Well . . . it was mostly Gail's idea."

"But you did it." And Tracy began to cry—not loudly as Charlie had, but silently, with huge tears running down her cheeks. "I didn't want to like you guys! I didn't want to have fun! I wanted to be miserable, and I wanted you all to be miserable with me!"

Dorian came and sat beside Tracy and held out her arms. Tracy fell into her hug and buried her face in Dorian's shoulder.

"Shannon," Dorian said as she stroked Tracy's hair, "I think it's time for the food."

We understood that she didn't want all of us staring at Tracy, so we forced ourselves to get busy eating. We had Doritos, potato chips, popcorn, and candy bars from the snack shop, though Cissy refused to give up her second Snickers. We also had lukewarm bug juice in paper cups.

I reached into my suitcase and pulled out my special surprise—eleven packages of slightly mashed chocolate Tastykakes. Everyone cheered wildly, and we ate ourselves silly. It's probably a good thing we hadn't won the pizza, or we'd have been sick as could be. Redwood had won. They could have the honor of being sick.

When we climbed into bed, it was well past lights out, but no one cared. It was the last night of camp for a whole year, and it was special—even if the campfire program had been rained out.

Now I lay on my bunk, warmed by memories

and waiting for the action I was sure was yet to come. I had almost fallen asleep when I heard someone moving about quietly. Then the door opened and closed.

Quickly I reached for my flashlight, slid to the floor, and reached for my sneakers. They were right where I'd left them. I rolled my pajama pants up above my knees and slipped my raincoat on. The material crackled so loudly in my ears that I expected everyone to sit up and tell me to go back to bed.

I tiptoed to the door and opened it quietly, then I stood on the porch and looked around. It was dark and difficult to see in the rain, even though the light at the edge of the field was on and the washhouse was lit as usual.

I went down the steps, afraid I'd lost my quarry already. The rain beating on my hood made it impossible to hear any sound but my own heart-beat. I stepped into a puddle and felt the water pour into my shoes. I thought longingly of my dry bed.

At that moment I saw her. She was over by the dining room and had turned her flashlight on for a second. Then she went around the corner of the building and out of sight.

She was going toward the creek. I hurried across the field and around the corner after her. At first I thought the wild roar that struck me was my own hammering heart. Then I realized with surprise that it was rushing, turbulent water. French Creek was going crazy!

I sloshed down to the creek, slipping in the mud once and going down on my bottom. My teeth clicked together with the force of the fall, and I felt the cold water seep through my pajamas. I picked myself up and squished on.

The only reason I saw her again was because her light-colored raincoat stood out against the dark, raging water. She was on the narrow wooden footbridge that led to Campfire Island.

She had reached the island and disappeared from view again by the time I reached the bridge. I grabbed the railing, stepped onto the walkway, and looked down in surprise. The bridge was quivering in my hand and under my feet as though it were alive.

The wild water was dashing itself against the bridge. I worried that the structure would come apart under me. I might be thoroughly wet, but I didn't want to take a midnight swim, especially not in this. I stared, hypnotized, at the white foam curling about my feet, lapping over the edge.

Then, even as I watched, the foaming stopped. I stared in confusion, then in fear. It had stopped because the water was no longer hurling itself against the side of the walkway—it was pouring in a sheet over the top, burying the bridge neatly beneath its surface.

I looked across the bridge. The island would be cut off any minute by the flooding creek. I had to get her back to Ponderosa while there was time!

But where was she?

I inched my way across the quaking bridge, using the railing for balance, feeling the force of the current against my ankles. I breathed a huge sigh of relief when I stepped onto the island.

Safe for the moment.

I walked to the campfire ring and turned a slow circle, searching the darkness for a light-colored raincoat. I didn't want to turn my flashlight on, because I didn't want to scare her. After all, she thought she was alone.

I threw my hood back and listened. Nothing. All I could hear was the water's furious rampage. I decided to leave the hood down just in case she screamed or something.

As the rain plastered my hair to my skull and

ran coldly down my back, I circled the island. Where was she? The island wasn't all that big. How could I miss her?

Once I stepped where there should have been island and felt water around my ankle. I pulled back and risked using my flashlight. The edge of the island was under water. It was obvious that the rising creek wasn't going to wait patiently for me to rescue anyone.

A shrill scream sounded to my left and scared me silly. I spun around and ran toward the sound.

There she was, back to a big tree, her flashlight shining on a wet and miserable skunk.

I stopped short. The last thing we needed was to set off a skunk's alarm system.

"Tracy! Are you all right?" I called.

Tracy looked over at me as though it were the most natural thing in the world to find me on Campfire Island in the middle of the night in a torrential rain.

"He brushed against my ankle," she explained. "I thought I'd die!"

I nodded. "He lives here."

She turned abruptly to the tree behind her, and her movement scared the skunk. It turned to run, lifting its tail and stamping its back feet in the process.

I hate even to drive by a long dead skunk on the road. All I can say is that I hope I am never again present when a very alive one performs. I gagged and coughed as the horrible odor filled the air. My eyes watered and burned, the tears washing down my cheeks with the rain.

Tracy was having a worse time than I was because she was closer to the little thing when it let loose. She wiped and wiped at her eyes and coughed and hacked and sputtered. She fanned the air, trying to make the smell go away, but of course it didn't.

Somebody told me once that tomato juice washes the skunk smell out of dogs who have gotten sprayed. I hoped it worked for people, too, and I hoped the camp kitchen had lots of the stuff, because Tracy and I were going to need it.

"We're stuck with the smell," I said. "Come on." I reached out my hand. "Let's get out of here."

She shook her head and turned back to the tree, shining her flashlight at a hole in the trunk. The hole was slightly higher than my waist.

"I'm trying to get the stuff out of here," she said. "I want to give it back."

I wasn't sure anyone would want it back if it smelled like we did, but I didn't say so.

"Why don't you come get it in the daytime? It would be a lot easier."

"I know, but then someone might see me. I didn't care when I brought the stuff, but I care now."

I knew I wouldn't want people to see me returning stuff I'd stolen, either. Too embarrassing.

"What's in there?" I asked, pointing to the hole.

"The Disney World sweatshirt and the beach towels. And I can't reach them!" The last was a cry.

"Let me try," I said.

"Shine the light down," she said, gesturing toward the ground. "The whole trunk's hollow."

I directed the light inside the tree, and there lay the sweatshirt and the towels looking amazingly dry. I reached into the tree for them. When my arm pit was pressed against the lower edge of the opening, I still had not touched anything.

"I can't reach the stuff, either," I said, pulling my arm out. "It's fallen down too far. And where's my fishing pole?" I shined the light back into the hole.

"Not in there," she said. "Here. I just leaned it against the tree."

I grabbed the rod with a smile and a sigh. I had my memories back.

"You brought this stuff here in the night, didn't you?" I asked, hugging the rod. "You sneaked out after we were all asleep."

I felt proud that I'd figured it out. That's why I'd stayed awake waiting. I figured if she had sneaked out before, she'd probably sneak out again. I'd follow her and—boom!—I'd have proof of guilt for Mrs. A.

But Tracy shook her head. "I never did anything at night, not after the first night when you scared me to death."

"I scared you? Well, you gave me the creeps!" I shivered at the memory, but I felt confused. I had been so certain I knew what had happened. I must remember never to become a private eye. "Then how'd the stuff get here?"

"I just brought it over in the day."

"Just like that? And no one stopped you or said anything?"

She shook her head. "Lots of girls walk around with fishing poles and towels."

"But lots of girls don't walk around on Campfire Island. We're not allowed here."

She grinned. "But who's to know you're here if you don't cross the bridge? That's where people see you. I just walked across the dam with the pole or

111

the towels or the shirt and walked upstream until I was across from the island. The creek's not that deep there. I waded across. At first I was just going to dump the stuff, but when I found this tree, I decided to use the hole as a hiding place."

"I can't believe no one saw you!"

"The front of the island is pretty open because of the bridge and the campfire ring and all, but the back is all shrubby. It's easy to duck if you need to. And I didn't care if any kids saw me. I just made sure no adults were looking when I waded over."

"It was pretty risky, you know," I said.

Tracy nodded. "I know. But I didn't care. All I wanted was to make trouble."

"Well, you did that. And we've got *big* trouble now," I said. "We've got to get back before someone notices we're gone or the island floods, whichever comes first. We'll have to get the stuff out of the tree tomorrow."

We turned and slogged as quickly as we could toward the bridge. I kept my flashlight trained on the ground in front of us. Tracy shone hers also, and she was the first one to find the bridge. She jerked back with shock at the sight of the water pouring over it and over the edges of the island.

"You go across, then I'll come," I said. "I don't

think the bridge will hold the two of us at once."

She nodded and walked forward cautiously. The rushing water grabbed at her legs as she stepped onto the bridge, but she clutched the railing firmly with both hands.

"Are you all right?" I called from my safe position at the water's edge.

She nodded, shuffling carefully along the bridge. She was as startled as I when the water suddenly swept her feet out from under her. She went down still hanging on to the railing. She looked like a sheet blowing on the clothesline on a very windy day.

"Help!" she screamed as she fought to get her feet back on the bridge. The force of the water pulled at her, its strength greater than hers. "Help!"

"Hold on, Tracy! Hold on!" I rushed to help her, but before I got to her, one section of the railing gave way. I watched in horror as she disappeared beneath the water.

"Tracy!" I screamed. I'd never been so scared in my life!

God, don't let her drown! Oh, God, help!

Suddenly she bobbed to the surface, clinging to a section of railing that was still attached to the bridge. It was the only thing that kept her from being swept away.

God, don't let it break loose! Please don't let it!

It was incredible to me that she was so close to me—just a few steps, really—but in so much danger. I had to help her!

"Here!" I yelled, thrusting my fishing pole at her. "Grab this!"

Between the darkness and her fear, she didn't see the pole at first. I waved it around, not so she'd see it, but hoping it would touch her.

Suddenly Tracy realized the pole was there, and she made a desperate one-handed lunge. Her fingers closed over the rod, slipped, then caught firmly on one of the threading eyelets.

She let go of the railing and grabbed the pole with both hands. The sudden weight of her body, coupled with the terrible tug of the water, almost dragged me in with her. I never expected that much pull, and I was terrified that the pole would slip out of my hands. I leaned back and held on as hard as I could.

I think I screamed when my feet slipped, and I sat with a jolt, half in and half out of the water. I tried to dig my heels in to keep myself steady, but they kept slipping in the mud.

A small but sturdy tree stump grew beside me. If I could just get behind it, it would keep me from being dragged into the current.

I shimmied along the ground on my bottom an inch at a time until I got to the stump. My arms ached and my shoulders felt like they'd explode from Tracy's weight. I wished she'd stop thrashing, but I knew she was fighting to keep her head out of the water as it tumbled her about.

When my foot found one of the stump's roots,

I pushed against it to test its strength. It held firm, and I used it to keep my feet from slipping. Slowly, carefully I slid behind the stump, feeling its permanence.

Tracy couldn't do anything to help herself. Holding on took all her strength. Getting her out of the water was up to me. If only I could reel her in the way I reeled in a fish!

I slid my left hand a couple of inches up the rod, then gripped tightly. Then I slid my right hand to meet my left. I repeated the hand maneuver again and yet again. Left up a few inches. Right a few inches to meet it. Left. Right. Left. Right. Slowly Tracy came closer and closer.

God, help her hold on! Help me hold on!

Suddenly the pressure on my arms was greatly reduced, and I almost fell over backwards. She'd let go! I struggled to my feet screaming, "Tracy!"

"Here," she yelled, almost at my feet. She was still in the water up to her chest, but she cried, "I'm kneeling!"

"Stand!" I ordered, reaching a hand to her. "Then we can get you on shore."

"I'm afraid! The water will grab me again!" But slowly she pulled herself erect in spite of the swirling, greedy water.

116

She was exhausted, and it wouldn't take much for her to fall. If she did, neither of us could go through this routine another time. Jelly arms and jelly legs would defeat us.

"Step toward me, Tracy! Take my hand! You can do it!"

She reached once, twice, then grabbed me with unbelievable strength. I leaned back, surprised, to pull better. My feet were out from under me again before I knew it.

I crashed painfully against the stump and lost my grip on both Tracy and the fishing pole.

"Shannon!" Her scream was filled with fear. I grabbed for her with both hands, catching her wrist and her raincoat just as, water whipping angrily about her knees, she began to lose her balance.

I pulled and she threw herself at the shore, and this time we were successful. We collapsed side by side, gasping and shaking and unbelievably weary.

I don't know how long we lay there panting and exhausted, but it was the water sliding under my head that warned me. I sat up and looked about in amazement. The island was no longer visible. It was completely under water.

"Tracy!" I scrambled to my feet. "Get up!"

"I can't," she whispered. "I can't."

"You have to!" I began dragging on her arm, pulling her. She was a dead weight. I bent down, gave her a great push, and she rolled over. As soon as her face hit the water, she came to her knees sputtering.

"The island's under water, Tracy! Get up! We've got to get higher!"

"Higher?" She pulled herself to her feet. "Up a tree?"

"That's the only higher I can think of."

We no longer had a flashlight. Tracy's went under with her in her fall, and mine had disappeared some time during the struggle to get her ashore. I tried to get my bearings, but it was weird with no land showing.

"There's a big beech tree somewhere around here," I said. "The branches start nice and low."

The water was above my ankles, and I could feel its pull. We had to find that tree, and fast. I knew we couldn't fight the flood. I just hoped we had energy enough to climb.

"Is that it?" asked Tracy, pointing wearily. "Hey, when did the rain stop?"

"I don't know." I looked up automatically, and sure enough, the rain was over. You'd think that would mean the water would start going down, but it wasn't working that way yet.

We slogged through the water to the beech tree as fast as we could.

"Climb!" I yelled and gave her a boost.

She started up, slipped, caught herself and started again. I was standing in shin-deep water when I put my right hand on a branch and pulled myself up after her.

"Keep going!" I yelled when she stopped too soon. "As high as you can possibly go."

When we finally stopped climbing, the branches were still strong enough to hold us, but only just. I leaned into the trunk, weak to the point of fainting.

I hurt. I was scared. I was wet and cold. I didn't know if the tree was high enough to keep us above the water. And my fishing pole was gone again, this time for good. Good-bye, memories.

For a long time the only noise was the roar of the creek. Then Tracy spoke.

"When did you know I was the thief?"

"Probably this afternoon," I said. "I'd wondered sooner, especially because of something Gail said, but I wasn't sure."

"What did she say?"

"We were talking about the things that had been taken, and she mentioned that they were things that could be grabbed quickly. Then your sweatshirt was taken. For that the thief would have had to go into your suitcase and search, and that was time consuming and risky. Either we had a new pattern, or you were trying to cover your tracks by appearing to be a victim too."

"I thought I was so clever when I took my own shirt," Tracy said.

"You were. It definitely confused things. I was especially mixed up when I saw Charlie pull the watch and Bible out of her suitcase. I even went to Mrs. A. about it."

"But you weren't convinced she'd stolen them?"

I shook my head. "Charlie's mouthy and mean sometimes, and I could believe she might take Leigh's watch. There was something to be gained from stealing a watch. But towels? And a fishing pole?"

I squirmed around, trying to find a place to lean without being stuck in the back by a knot or a branch.

I continued. "When Charlie explained why she had been in my suitcase earlier in the week, I knew you must be the culprit."

"But you still made me that wonderful gift."

"I didn't want you to stay a thief!"

"Neither do I."

"But Tracy, why did you try to frame Charlie?" I thought this was the meanest thing Tracy had done all week.

"I didn't try to frame her," Tracy said. "I put the things in her suitcase, but I never told anyone they were there. I just wanted to give Charlie a hard time because she's so strong."

"But she's not," I said.

"I know that now," said Tracy. "I guess I just wanted to hurt her."

I rested my head against a branch, and next thing I knew, the sky was turning light. I wondered how long I had slept. I yawned and stretched and looked down.

"Wow!" I was filled with awe.

Water rushed in brown satin sheets beneath me. Where it battered itself against our tree, it foamed white. Branches and all sorts of junk whirled past in the current. What looked like a door swept by, with a sad looking raccoon crouched on it.

"I wonder what happened to our skunk," I said.

"Three guesses." Tracy's voice sounded as exhausted as she looked.

I twisted on my branch so that I could look at Harmony Hill in the ever brighter light. It looked funny from up so high, but the strangest sight was the dining room. Most of it was under water, and the field by the cabins was a wading pool. Everything else looked fine.

As we watched, Mrs. A. and Miss Martha came out of Main House and began wading across the field to the dining room. We started waving and shouting, but the leaves on the tree were so thick, it took forever before they saw us. I don't think they ever did hear us above the flood.

Tracy and I were rescued by volunteer firemen
who shot a line gun across the creek to our tree.
First they shot a thin rope. Then we had to pull
and pull the thin rope until a thick rope attached
to it reached us. We wrapped and wrapped this
rope around the tree because it would have lots of
pressure on it.

A man then came for us in an inflatable boat
that was actually attached to the rope so it couldn't
get swept away. The man pulled the boat across the
creek hand over hand. He tied the rope to the tree
the way it was supposed to be tied, and then he
took us back, left hand, right hand, left hand, right
hand.

Mrs. A. was angry and relieved when we finally

reached safety, and she couldn't decide which she was most. I was just glad I was rescued before Mom came to take me home. If I'm super sensitive since Dad left, she's even worse. Seeing me sitting up in that tree would have been hard on her.

It was hard to say good-bye to the New Jersey girls and Leigh and Cissy. It was very hard to say good-bye to Tracy. Now that she was turning out to be an okay person, we wouldn't see each other anymore.

"Just remember that God loves you even when people fail," I said.

Tracy was standing by her grandmother's car. Her mother and Harry wouldn't be home for a few more days.

She nodded. "I'll try and remember," she said. She climbed in and drove out of my life.

I hoped she'd let God get close to her, because the problem with her mom and Horrible Harry was still there.

"Yo, Shannon!" It was Charlie, leaning out the window of the Andersons' car. "See you around!"

"Sure will! Like at church tomorrow!" I waved and climbed into our car.

It was good to see Mom again.

"So tell me," she said as we drove away. "Did

you have a good week in spite of being apart from your friends?"

I smiled. "I made new friends," I said.

"I thought you would," Mom said. "Aren't you glad you stayed?"

I nodded. I had not only made new friends, I had made new memories. I lost a few too, I guess, when my fishing rod was washed downstream, but maybe that's good. I needed to remember God's sure love more than my Dad's poor love.

"It was a great week," I said. "Hooray, Ponderosa."

Then I leaned my head back and slept.

Here's what girls like you are saying about the East Edge Mysteries!

"I love the suspense. I'd like to read more about Dee."
—Melissa, 12

"I like it that the girls are a normal group of girls. It is interesting to read about kids like you."—Kendra, 10

"The books are fast to read and you can finish them in a short time. That's just what I like."—Amy, 13

Be sure to read about Charlie's adventures in East Edge #4 *The Case of the Missing Melody*

I couldn't believe it! Mom was going to California with some bald guy named Dink—what kind of a dumb name is Dink?—and she was leaving me behind. And she was happy!

I felt like I had a knife in my heart. I felt like I was dying.

Where did this Dink person come from? I'd never heard of him before, so she must have just met him.

She's going to California with some bearded stranger, and she's leaving me behind. She's leaving me behind!

"Never get involved with babies, Charlie," Mom always told me. "They mess up your life."

I'd always thought she meant babies in general, little weepy, sniveling kids, the ones you see crabbing in the grocery store. But she hadn't. She'd meant me.